Literary
Allsorts

Literary Allsorts

A COLLECTION OF SHORT STORIES

Barbara Shrubsole

Copyright © 2016 Barbara Shrubsole

The moral right of the author has been asserted.

Apart from any fair dealing for the purposes of research or private study, or criticism or review, as permitted under the Copyright, Designs and Patents Act 1988, this publication may only be reproduced, stored or transmitted, in any form or by any means, with the prior permission in writing of the publishers, or in the case of reprographic reproduction in accordance with the terms of licences issued by the Copyright Licensing Agency. Enquiries concerning reproduction outside those terms should be sent to the publishers.

This is a work of fiction. Names, characters, businesses, places, events and incidents are either the products of the author's imagination or used in a fictitious manner. Any resemblance to actual persons, living or dead, or actual events is purely coincidental.

Matador
9 Priory Business Park,
Wistow Road, Kibworth Beauchamp,
Leicestershire. LE8 0RX
Tel: 0116 279 2299
Email: books@troubador.co.uk
Web: www.troubador.co.uk/matador
Twitter: @matadorbooks

ISBN 978 1785892 097

British Library Cataloguing in Publication Data.
A catalogue record for this book is available from the British Library.

Printed and bound by CPI Group (UK) Ltd, Croydon, CR0 4YY
Typeset in 11pt Aldine401 BT by Troubador Publishing Ltd, Leicester, UK

Matador is an imprint of Troubador Publishing Ltd

This book is dedicated to my friends Val and Sharon Pile in the hope that they will accept it in place of the novel they have encouraged me to write.

Contents

An Introduction	ix
Bread	1
Caught	5
The Red Letter Day	10
Unforgettable Fragrance	18
Seeing is Believing	25
And the Name is "Smith"	32
Tulips From Amsterdam	38
The Seagull	44
The Surprise Package	52
A Heavy Load	57
Pen Friends	64
The Rainbow-Coloured Scarf	68
Who's Afraid of the Big Bad Wolf?	74
No Future in the Past	80
All on a Summer's Day	85
Called to Account	90
Mix and Match	95
A Very Nice Man	105
The Meeting	110
On Special Offer	117
And as a Post Script…	129

An Introduction

Welcome to my collection of short stories.
Where to begin?

The first story in the book has been carefully chosen because it is my favourite and it can be said to be my greatest claim to writing fame (however limited) in that others also liked it. Hopefully it will encourage you to read more.

Where does inspiration come from?

The simple answer…people, places and experiences… just about anything may spark off an idea that then flickers or flames into life.

I have tried to work out an order for the contents but it is difficult to categorise the stories in any way. Suffice to say this book is a mixture of stories that have emerged over several years and I have decided to put them into print rather than leave them hidden in a computer file. Occasionally you may note that one idea has ignited more than one follow up story. In some way my belief that 'people need to meet people' is pursued, in this case, via the written page.

I have also come to believe that there may well be in everyone the innate desire to continue the work of creation. This can be brought to life in all sorts of ways and take a variety of forms. For me, at this moment, it is seen in short story writing and you are now part of my attempt to live out this belief.

The majority of stories have a conclusion but I hope that a question as to what might happen next could, in some cases, surface during the reading.

The collection concludes with a story that involves a number of people brought together for a celebration. I hope that you will be able to stay with me throughout the book and find enjoyment in your reading just as I have found pleasure in telling the stories.

Finally, I thank all those who, without knowing, have prompted a story and also those who have given me encouragement and practical help in bringing this book to life.

Bread

Nancy Ingram folded the foil round the pile of bank-notes. The decision had been made and she intended to stick with it. She carefully placed the mini silver brick in the white carrier bag.

The excitement was clear in the two bright eyes that smiled back at her from the hall mirror.

She tucked the soft purple scarf neatly inside the collar of her closely fitting coat and pulled her hat well down over her ears.

"And there's no one now to tell me what I can or can't do!"

She addressed her reflection with an air of defiance. Any other day, she might have added that the loneliness was something else, but this afternoon Nancy's thoughts were very positive.

Bus pass safely pocketed, gloves on, and, struggling to control her umbrella, Nancy, plus bag of goodies, was off to catch the 2.40 into town.

Where would Harry be today? She had come to quite enjoy the challenge of locating him…it might be tricky today as he would have chosen somewhere out of the rain if he had any sense.

Nancy didn't know the real name of this young man who, five months ago, had suddenly become a part of her life. A chance happening? Some people would say it was meant to be but Nancy remained open minded. All she knew was that she did not shop on Sundays out of principle but on that occasion she had chosen to take a short cut across the precinct on her way to the central churches' tea. Somehow her attention had been drawn to the young man seated with his back to the wall, begging receptacle at the ready. Despite being clearly very 'down and out,' he reminded her of Harry… that other Harry who might have… but all that was a long time ago.

From that first encounter, the 'now' Harry had continued to bother Nancy, not physically but emotionally. He had probably been like any one of the small children she had taught, full of hope and expectation. What had happened? Over the weeks her vivid imagination had created a variety of scenarios provoking a mixture of anger and tears. Nancy's simple response was, however, the provision of a regular Sunday bag of food. Not that she received any sign of gratitude, but that didn't matter.

"But it's not enough," her conscience nagged at her, "sandwiches, fruit and homemade cake won't get him out of this mess!"

He needed money. She had money.

She'd made a bold decision.

That morning Jason got very wet before he sat down. He chose his spot carefully. The roof overhang provided some protection and he was out of the wind.

He never made any effort to tidy himself these days, he slept in his clothes, and he did not smell nice.

Sunday sympathy shoppers were the best… even better

when he'd had Harley. Funny how people responded to dogs! He missed Harley. He missed lots of things!

The day passed slowly. With a degree of regularity, coins dropped into the battered cap, just as he had expected... there was certainly one plus about rotten weather... people felt more sorry for you.

By mid afternoon he was sure he'd done pretty well. He was contemplating leaving when the white carrier bag came into view.

Nancy had guessed right. The rain had nearly stopped and she actually found him easily.

Jason was surprised to see the old bat out on such a miserable afternoon... you'd got to hand it to her, she was persistent.

He watched as she crossed the precinct towards him. Chin resting on bent knees, he always found it best to avoid eye contact. The feet stopped just in front of him. Goodness they were small. He hadn't realised quite how skinny her legs were. Bet those shoes cost a bit. Bloody 'do-gooders" made him so mad!

What did she know? Warm comfortable home and family. Even his Great Aunt Vera had gone and died when he needed her most. It wasn't fair!

In the past, he'd resisted the urge to tell her just what he thought of her ruddy triangle sandwiches and bananas. He lived in the Night Shelter not the bloody Ritz! Even getting angry was an effort now. The past months seemed to have sapped his spirit.

The bag was beside him and she was off. Had he murmured a 'Thank you?' ... Probably not. He watched as she made her way across to the corner and disappeared.

He'd never really noticed how she moved before… strange how someone her age could appear so confident. Would he ever find confidence again? Why not? Perhaps he might try a shower this evening and maybe he could get some new underwear from the store cupboard. What if that student with the red hair was serving supper tonight?

But just as quickly negative thoughts replaced the positive as reality returned.

He shivered. It was definitely time to move.

It was time also for the 139 to make its way back up the hill.

Nancy Ingram, seated with hands clasped loosely in her lap, gazed out of the window into the darkness, and wondered.

Jason stood up. He was stiff. He stretched his aching back, flexed his knees, walked to the nearby litterbin and tipped in the contents of the white carrier bag. The strong bag would act as his portable safe as usual.

It was on Monday, October 3rd, at 7.27am precisely, that, due to natural curiosity, David Spriggs, refuse collector, discovered something that would make a considerable difference in his life!

Caught

He first saw the butterfly when it landed on the second step up from the grass, near where he was sitting. It stayed there for a few seconds and then flew to the purple flowers.

Michael got up to have a closer look. He'd seen many butterflies before, but somehow this one seemed larger and brighter.

It fluttered from flower to flower pausing briefly in the centre of each blossom.

"Suppose it's getting some sort of food," Michael thought, "Stands a pretty good chance of overeating in this garden!"

He smiled. Not a common occurrence in recent days.

Michael had been living with his grandparents for nearly a year.

When his Mum and Dad split up it had felt like the end of the world. He'd guessed it would happen. Every night he had prayed for a miracle. In the stories he'd heard when they used to go to church there was nothing about parents splitting up but some fantastic things happened so he had kept trying.

It hadn't worked.

Mum had said, "It will be best if you go and stay with

Gran and Granddad for a while. You do understand don't you?"

He had wanted to shout, "Oh yes! I understand only too well. More than you realise. I know I'm just a nuisance."

He had remained silent. He had no choice.

Michael loved Gran and Granddad and he could see that they were hurt already and he didn't want to add to their unhappiness.

Mum had her work. Dad had…other things. It was obvious. He was just in the way.

He saw his parents fairly often… separately. It felt like some sort of pretend game.

The butterfly moved to the rocks at the edge of the pond. The patterns on the wings showed up clearly as it rested on the pale stone.

Michael knew that there had never been any fish in the pond but what fun it had been 'fishing' with the cousins when they had all come on family visits. The garden had seemed so exciting, so many opportunities for climbing and jumping. The lawn had been quite big enough for cricket and Dad had …

Edward and Fiona's mum and dad were still together.

The butterfly was on Gran's wheelbarrow now. How would it like the taste of those flowers?

They were different… all sorts of colours. Michael wished the old butter churn hadn't fallen to pieces.

The wheelbarrow wasn't quite the same.

Nothing was the same.

The butterfly seemed happy enough, enjoying the sun before deciding where to go to next.

Michael's pad lay on the grass.

Under the heading 'FLIGHT' Michael had begun to work at the homework suggested by Mr Johns in, what was described as, the "Creative Writing" lesson.

Mr Johns was a bright area in Michael's life.

Mr Johns understood about Michael… a nine year old boy for whom just living was so hard. No two circumstances are the same but Mr Johns had been there. And he understood.

The class topic at the moment centred on flying. There was no compulsory homework but Mr Johns believed in cultivating the habit of making good use of your time.

Gran had supported the project with photographs taken during her hot air balloon trip and Granddad had helped him make a glider.

Mr Johns said, "Creative Writing needs more than pen and paper."

That's why Michael had decided to work in the garden, taking crisps and Coke with him to aid his thought processes.

"Give yourself time," Mr Johns' words. "Allow it to flow… and anything can happen."

Trouble was how to move his thinking from one area that filled his mind and got in the way of everything else.

"Plenty of action and don't forget dialogue." Mr Johns always treated you in a grown up way using the proper words. Michael liked that.

He was suddenly filled with a tremendous desire to catch the butterfly.

The glass. He emptied the last drops of Coke and gave it a shake. Now the cardboard off the back of the pad. It was a bit large but it would do.

Dad had showed him how to get rid of an unwanted bee from the house. Same process should work.

He would wait till it landed on a stone or the path.

It was back amongst its favourite purple flowers.

He stood and gazed at it. The wings were so large for such a small body.

Wings placed together now as it settled, a flutter, then still again. This creature demanded his full attention.

Michael waited…

Momentarily his mind wandered and the concentration on the butterfly was replaced by thoughts of Harrier Jump Jets. They'd watched a video of an air show and then another about insects.

"Man has terrific potential for discovery through nature," Mr Johns had said.

Michael hadn't been quite sure what it meant but it sounded important.

The butterfly took off and landed on a stone, its wings spread wide displaying its full beauty.

Michael approached carefully. One false move and it would be off.

He lowered the glass, gently now, nearer, nearer and down. It was over the butterfly.

Slide the card underneath.

It was trapped.

Michael stood up and held the prisoner in front of his face. He watched as the frantic creature beat its wings against the sides of the glass. No freedom of flight now. Its world was reduced to this confined space with no means of escape.

"Use your imagination." He heard Mr Johns' voice clearly inside his head.

The butterfly was out of the glass now and in his hand.

"I hate you!" Michael said.

He repeated the words six times, as slowly and sadistically he pulled off its legs, one by one.

And finally, tearing apart the wings, he scattered all the bits among the purple flowers, turned, and walked purposefully towards the house.

The Red Letter Day

"You're hurting me Mummy."

Kelly was holding his hand very tightly as she dragged him along. She kept glancing round. They were on their way home but she always felt uneasy out on her own in the dark. Thankfully the 'head and table confrontation' had proved far from life-threatening. The 'lots of blood' that Joseph had told the nurse about had come from a fairly small cut and any further blood flow was blocked by three butterfly strips.

They'd been nice. Nobody suggested a lack of care on her part. The whole place had felt warm and welcoming but all she wanted now was to get back home as quickly as possible.

Joseph had been so brave. Why take her problems out on him?

She loosened her grip a little.

"Sorry love, but we must be back before Santa comes."

What a way to spend Christmas Eve!

As they rounded the corner Kelly's worst fears were confirmed. She saw the group near the gate. She knew it was the regular meeting place for some of the troublemakers from the flats but she'd hoped it would be different tonight.

Four hours ago everything had been fine. Now she was dead scared and desperate to reach the safety of the flat.

The entrance was barred.

"So what's with you then Kel? Not like you to be out after dark!"

His mates joined in the fun.

"That lad of yours should be in bed." With an added, "So should his mother!"

"Mustn't miss Father Christmas."

"Only father he's likely to see!" More laughter.

The first guy held a bottle in front of her.

"How about we share a bit of Christmas cheer together? We can take it in turns unless you fancy something different."

"Give us a chance to wish you a Happy Christmas!" The black guy started a chorus of 'We Wish You a Merry Christmas,' which rapidly increased in volume as the others joined in.

Kelly fought back the tears. What could she do Joseph was pressed up close against her. He was obviously scared of what was happening. She had to get him inside.

"Cut that f****** racket or I'll give you something to sing about." Immediate silence. Nobody deliberately offended 'Giant Haystacks,' the name he'd been given by everyone in the flats. The massive body filled the doorway of his flat just across from the gate.

In a moment Kelly's immediate problems melted away and she was alone, and free to move through the gate and up to her flat.

Once inside she felt a bit better. She paused to fasten the chain and lock the door.

Joseph rushed on ahead into the lounge. Kelly followed surprisingly aware, as her hand moved to the switch, of how the tiny silver tree in the corner caught something of the light from the outside streetlamp.

"He hasn't been yet." Joseph clutched the still very empty striped sock. They had solved the problem of no fireplace and hence no chimney by agreeing to place the waiting receptacle so that it was clearly visible from the window fortunately accepted by Joseph as the obvious place of entry. The sock had actually been 'hung up' just after noon.

Joseph unzipped and removed his own anorak.

Then followed a non-stop barrage of words in a rather one-sided conversation.

"I'm hungry. Can I have some crisps? He will come won't he? I'm so excited. Don't hurt me! I'm hungry!"

Kelly responded with an occasional, yes, no or a grunt of assent as if on 'automatic pilot.' She proceeded with the bedtime routine that on this occasion began with carefully easing the blood spattered T-shirt over his head.

"Don't forget the carrot!" As if she could!

At length, hunger appeased, and with vital refreshments for future visitors in place in the vicinity of the window, one small boy was safely tucked up in bed with the clear direction that he must go to sleep quickly or Santa might not come. Amazing how the earlier accident had ceased to feature now in his joyful anticipation of the day ahead.

Joyful anticipation was completely absent as an emotionally drained young woman gratefully sank down in the welcoming cushions of the armchair. She would have some time to wait before her next role of assisting Santa.

The room seemed so dull after the brightness of the 'Walk In' centre. "Merry Christmas" the banner had said... nothing very merry about her life. There were several people in the waiting room when they'd arrived. Joseph had held on to her while she completed information with the receptionist but once they were sat down he had treated the guy seated next to them like a long lost friend, telling him all about how he'd fallen over Dillon's bowl and that he'd hung up one of his longest socks for Santa. He seemed to have forgotten about the 'tea towel bandage,' (a memory from first aid at school) that had been wrapped round his head.

Kelly had been a bit surprised, somewhat embarrassed, when they were called in ahead of people who'd been there before them, actually quite in order due to them being a 'blood case' as the nurse informed her. She'd made matters worse when her 'hold everything' bag had spilled its contents between the chairs as she'd got up. Joseph's new found friend had helped her gather everything up.

It was only now, when the whole episode was over and things restored to normal, that she gave way.

It wasn't fair! She'd tried so hard. Heaven knows it hadn't been easy. Several times she'd nearly given up. Alone... always alone to make decisions. The leaders at the nursery said Joseph was fine. She'd felt so proud being his Mum. A few Dads had been at the nativity thing. She'd managed to conquer the tears that threatened to break through. It wouldn't be long before Joseph would start asking difficult questions about his Dad. Questions... so many questions and no one to help with the answers.

Her son's latest photograph looked down from its pride of place on the cabinet. The same blue eyes and tangled curls... no doubting his parentage.

"Your father is shit... utter shit."

She never allowed herself to use this sort of language when Joseph was around but her anger just boiled over.

Then, in a moment of defiance, she added, "But he's not going to mess us two up!"

Kelly stood up and walked into her bedroom.

Joseph's presents were hidden in the back corner of her bedroom cupboard, out of reach of any inquisitive fingers. Most gifts had come from charity shops. She'd wrapped each one carefully in paper bought in the precinct.

Cupboard door opened, she moved some hangers aside and... met up again with the dress. She knew it was there, tucked away at the back of the rail. Kelly lifted it out and held it at arm's length.

Memories...

Suddenly she was gripped by an overwhelming desire to put it on. In a trice it was done. She sat down at her dressing table. Where were the earrings? Once fixed, the dangling stones caught the light creating several mini rainbows. Hands behind her neck, she grasped her hair and swept it high up on her head. Everything about her reflection confirmed that the 'lady in red' still had what it takes.

Then she was up and twirling around the confined

bedroom space and on into the lounge, music pounding inside her head. She was transported out of a rundown council flat into a land of dreams. All sense of tiredness left her limbs, depression evaporated, as she danced among the stars, lost to the world. The spirit that had remained caged for so long was suddenly set free.

Eventually, when her energy did run out, she collapsed back into the armchair.

A few minutes later, or it may have been longer, the sharp rattle of the letter box returned her dramatically to the here and now.

Horror! Who the…

Her mind flew back to the earlier incident.

Kelly froze. They'd come back to find her, to celebrate Christmas like they'd said. Perhaps if she kept quiet they'd go away. She wanted to scream.

"There's somebody at the door Mummy."

Oh no! What was he doing up?

"Why aren't you asleep?" The words fell out.

"I just needed a wee," and as Kelly showed no sign of moving from the chair, "aren't you going to open the door?" If only life always held the simplicity of a 4year old.

Joseph walked into the kitchen and obviously using his usual vantage point, called, "It's a policeman. I can see him through the window."

Police! What now? Not more trouble!

Didn't they even leave you alone on Christmas Eve?

But, whatever he wanted, Kelly at least felt less threatened. She turned the key and, keeping the safety chain in place, she opened the door a little.

Aware of the anxious face in the narrow opening the policeman spoke in reassurance.

"Nothing to be worried about… I'm Andy…we met earlier at the "Walk In" centre. You remember, Joseph told me about the cat and I helped with your bag.

I found an envelope under the chair. It looks important. I had to pass…"

She could see him through the gap.

"But I didn't…"

"… realise I was in the police." He finished the sentence for her.

"I had to get an enormous splinter dealt with before I came on duty."

She unhooked the chain. What a relief.

Andy stepped forward and passed her the envelope but before she could say anything Joseph took over.

He pushed her aside, caught hold of his new friend's hand and pulled him towards the lounge.

"Come and see Dillon. He's asleep on the settee." Then as an apparent afterthought, "Are you really a policeman?"

A smile passed between the two adults.

Embarrassment suddenly overtook Kelly for the second time today.

She was still wearing the red dress. God! Whatever would he think?

As if on cue Joseph came to her rescue.

"I'm a bit late getting to sleep 'cos I needed a wee and I'm too excited about Christmas. We're going to have sausages, chips and beans for dinner tomorrow. Mummy let me choose. And candles! You can come too if you like."

"Afraid not… maybe another day."

Joseph didn't appear to be expecting an answer because he just continued,

"I'm going to be a policeman when I grow up. Can you show me where…"

Kelly gently placed a hand over her son's mouth in an attempt to stem the never-ending flow.

The hand was quickly pulled aside.

"But he's my friend Mummy!"

This time it was Andy who came to the rescue.

The eyes of the six foot policeman met the expectant face of the small boy and responded.

"I've got an idea."

He reached into an inside pocket.

"How about coming to our special children's party on Wednesday?" He held out two cards. "One ticket for you and one for Mummy. And now I must get back on duty."

Another smile… then he was gone.

She shut the door, and, as if wanting to hold on to a surprise new feeling, very slowly completed the security and somewhat reluctantly turned back into reality.

"You look beautiful Mummy. Red's my best colour too."

Two steps and she gathered him up in her arms and, with his warm cheek against her bare shoulder, together they danced into the joy of Christmas.

Unforgettable Fragrance

The door closed behind Peter.

The invitation to join him in the States for a break had been too good to miss. Three days at work for him and three days just for me with the competition date pressing… uninterrupted writing, or only interrupted by things I wanted to do. Staying at Lindfield Suites allowed so much freedom.

A shower, a slice of toast, and, with a second mug of coffee beside me, I was ready to go. I had an idea and time to explore it.

I was away.

Little did I know of the story that would actually unfold around me.

I got so engrossed with Deirdre and Michael that I had no notion of time passing.

A draught of cold air caused me to look up.

I'd completely forgotten about room service. I knew the routine, well what had happened two years previously.

The large black woman stood there with her trolley. She returned my smile and went straight upstairs with an armful of towels.

Concentration broken, I decided on a coffee break. I'd make it before she needed to start on the kitchen area.

I was on the settee with coffee and book before she came down. She didn't seem to want to establish eye contact but there wasn't any way that I could avoid taking in the picture before me… the red, green and purple thigh clinging shorts that protruded below the massive T-shirt and the, more than ample bosom, displaying a riot of garden flowers. I mentally marked her as a future character somewhere.

'Blossom.' The name flashed into my mind. I smiled as I inwardly put words into her mouth. "What you see is what you get."

Might make a good slogan for that T-shirt, front or back!

It was very obvious that she did not want to join in conversation, so I returned to my reading.

The smell of the room freshener reached my nostrils. I glanced up and realised 'Blossom' had gone. Lovely perfume, much nicer than the 'over the top' stuff I've got at home. Whatever was it? So familiar and yet I couldn't pin it down.

My allocated reading of one chapter extended to three. Veronica Short had got me again. How did she always exert this magnetic power on me? The desperate need to know what would happen next!

I'd intended a daily 'fitness improving' swim but I'd start tomorrow.

Promises! Promises!

No… a definite decision to get back to Deirdre and Michael or should he be Mike?

As I reread my previous scribbling, the thought occurred to me that, considering her size, 'Blossom' had been incredibly quiet going about her work. I couldn't even recall hearing the door open or shut. Perhaps I should be writing a detective novel with this level of observation.

Back to the task in hand.

There followed a very positive afternoon's work, the only distraction when my space was invaded by the sound of a child crying somewhere nearby. It sounded so distressed. I felt somewhat irritated. Why was it that families couldn't even keep the peace on holiday?

It was only later that this sound took on a rather different significance.

When Peter returned he briefly asked about the day, and, without waiting for an answer of any length, went straight up for a shower. He called down something about my having had a swim and not using one of the beach towels and the white one being rather messy.

"But I…" My response was drowned by the noise of the shower.

We'd been invited out for drinks with a group of the American friends and time was limited.

Once in the bathroom it was only too clear what Peter was on about. One of the towels was very wet and marked with a dark stain.

I hadn't been upstairs since early morning. Something must have gone wrong during the cleaning. 'Blossom' should have said something. It was surprising because from previous experience personal service had been faultless.

Thursday started well.

I was determined to make use of the pool. I set the time. Clear plan.

Two hours writing and then outside for a break.

Michael and Deirdre were getting it all together. My story was moving along but I needed to remain conscious of holding any possible reader. It was all getting rather too predictable.

Time out.

I gathered the necessary together. What a nuisance needing reading glasses now. Perhaps I should invest in a tinted pair to avoid balancing sunglasses over them. Book, sun-cream and my own towel.

Nobody else there. Lovely. My concentrated effort produced a few lengths and then I settled myself to read. I was well and truly hooked. How is it that some writers take you over?

As I sat up, preparing to move my legs out of the direct sun, I saw that I was no longer alone.

A small black girl, aged I guessed about ten, was swimming up and down, diving under the water, twisting and turning. Her multicoloured costume gave her the appearance of an exotic fish. I'm not generally given to bouts of envy but did I feel envious as I watched her obvious delight at being in the water. What a good job she'd missed my laboured earlier efforts!

Aware of the dangers nowadays in being seen talking to children, I risked a smile as she approached the end where I was sitting but she seemed to be far away.

I returned to my reading.

When I next looked up she had gone. The thought

crossed my mind that it might have been her I'd heard crying… it certainly hadn't sounded like a baby.

The heat eventually forced me back inside.

As I opened the door the same lovely perfume greeted me. Whatever was it? I must ask Peter this evening although his sense of smell is not too hot.

I will allow you, the reader, to move on rapidly with me through the rest of the day since, enjoyable as it was for me, it has no bearing on what is to follow except perhaps to mention that the sound of crying violated my space again.

Time passed bringing with it a new day and my increased desire to renew the contact of pen with paper.

My story was coming along. The relationship was not all sweetness and light. Mike had passed the test with Deirdre's parents but I was poised to introduce the unexpected twist. The luxury of time for writing was paying off. I must try to build this space into my life back home.

I also had time for a swim today.

I felt a whole new positive attitude developing.

The mermaid was there again as I arrived poolside. She was wearing a white costume today, so stark against her dark skin.

I'd wait until she'd finished. It seemed almost obscene to share the pool with her.

As I watched my attention was drawn to her back. Lines. They looked like scar lines. I hadn't noticed before. Perhaps it had been due to the design of the costume.

I turned away. I felt quite sick but I couldn't resist looking again.

As she swam away from me the lines became clearer. They looked just like… scars made by a whip.

Cotton plantation slaves!

Everything about me froze, to such an extent that I didn't notice her leave the pool or where she went. Suffice to say, that when I came to, she had gone.

I couldn't face swimming after that. I just wanted to get back inside as quickly as possible. I let myself in and hardly noticed 'Blossom' as we passed on the bend of the stairs. I sought the comfort of a warm bath. I think I told her of my intention but it wasn't until I was soaking in a sea of bubbles that I acknowledged the ease with which we had passed considering her size and the stair space.

I made the decision to keep all this to myself until the right moment sometime later. It wasn't fair to bother Peter after three days' meetings and with a long drive ahead.

As I was packing, another thought struck me… there hadn't been a sound at the pool, not even the slightest splash.

I suddenly felt very cold.

And hell! What was that smell?

I waited in the foyer as Peter completed the necessary documentation.

I was quite glad we were moving on. The morning's happenings had really upset me. I couldn't get the picture out of my mind. Should I have done something? Quite honestly, I didn't want to get involved and yet I couldn't leave it alone.

The pain! Who had done it?

I was brought back to the here and now as I heard the receptionist say, "So sorry you were without a room cleaner during your stay. I hope you weren't too inconvenienced. We have real trouble recruiting workers now."

Ten minutes later, driving towards Jacksonville, I could restrain myself no longer.

"What did she mean about the cleaner?"

With eyes fixed ahead Peter told me that some months earlier one of the cleaners had committed suicide following the death of her daughter.

"You see," he said "the little girl was found floating in the pool. There were flowers on her body in the shape of a cross. Quite bizarre!"

And suddenly I knew.

"Freesias," I said quietly.

Seeing is Believing

The journey was nearly over. Ben's mood remained low key. He glanced at his watch. The guys would probably be at the airport, perhaps even on board, about to take to the skies while he was traversing the, all too familiar, roads of Somerset.

"Go on! Break the habit of a lifetime."

He had chickened out. Somehow he couldn't cope with Mum and Dad's disappointment of his not being there at the traditional Christmas family gathering, it being his birthday as well. He knew it would come one day but 2006 was too soon. The same routine, the same people and the same jokes? Did Christmas always have to be the same?

Miles away in thought, but thankfully fully awake he rounded the well-known bend and slammed on the brakes.

A mirage! It had to be. No, she was real all right, jumping up and down.

Thank goodness she was dressed in red…well, bits of her anyway… so that he'd easily seen her in the middle of the road.

God, those legs go on forever!

His eye travelled upwards past the exposed central area and took in the long blonde hair.

"Calm down. Get a hold of yourself." An inner voice of reason struggling to exert control.

Ben moved the car to the side of the road, turned off the engine, wound down the window and found himself in close proximity to a pair of sparkling blue eyes

"Thank goodness you saw me."

"You can say that again!" Was that the inner voice or his own thoughts this time?

"I need a lift."

"And some more clothes! Ask her what she's doing here. This is December… Not June!"

"Where do you want to get to?" The cool air was beginning to reduce Ben's rapidly rising temperature but reason was nowhere in sight.

"The Inn at Chew. Sorry…Chew Magna…I think the locals forget the Magna bit."

"Ask her what she's doing here." Same inner voice again, totally ignored.

"No trouble. I'm headed that way." Ben realised this was an inane comment as anyone travelling this road had very little chance of not passing Chew.

Exterior calm… interior in turmoil.

He leaned across, slid the two carrier bags on to the floor, and opened the passenger door.

"I'll just get Ben. You don't mind dogs do you? He won't be any trouble." And not waiting for an answer, she disappeared into the bushes.

A Christmas bird, with a dog called Ben, wanting a lift

in the already well-filled Metro of a psychology student named Ben.

"I don't believe it!" At this moment Ben quite happily aligned himself with a comment of his Granddad's generation.

He had a sudden urge to slam the door shut and drive off at top speed but... too late...the lady in red emerged from the greenery with Ben.

Given more time, man Ben might have speculated on dog Ben's breed but he would have undoubtedly failed to arrive at what now stood before him. Suffice to say, it was large and hairy with floppy ears and a tail that was in perpetual motion. It sort of bounced towards the car obviously able to see where it was going even though no eyes were visible.

A wet nose protruded through the open doorway.

"Let me introduce you. Ben say hello to..." she giggled, "I don't even know your name."

"It's Ben." Bet that surprised her! "And you are?"

"Amanda, but everyone, except my Dad, calls me Mandy."

A few minutes later an acquiescent Ben, was once more on the move but now in the newly acquired role of taxi driver.

Mandy had taken over. Black bags of washing, books and files, the flowers, his waterproof coat and all the other things he'd thrown in at the last moment had miraculously been reduced in space so as to make room for the four-legged traveller and in no time Mandy was seated beside him.

He glanced in the rear mirror. The dog was sitting

boldly upright, nose in the air, his outline framed by the pale tinges of the watery setting sun. He exuded the air of superiority and Ben decided to just get on with it, even if, from observation, his only decent jacket was in great danger of arriving at its destination covered in dog's hair.

But it was far from easy to concentrate on driving!

His thoughts ranged between total disbelief at what was happening, comments he might expect from his mates and whether he should actually tell his Mum anything at all. He was constantly brought back to the here and now by those legs trying so hard to distract him.

They travelled in silence for a while and then, "Atishoo!"

"Bless you!"

"Thanks."

"Atishoo!"

"Bless you!"

"It's usually about ten once I start so… Atishoo… you can forget the blessing."

He omitted to add that it was probably the dog's hair causing the problem.

"We're used to blessing in our house, my Dad's a vicar."

"Atishoo!" "Atishoo!" Fortunately the sneezing prevented any other explosive response from Ben.

Ben, the dog, started a whining noise.

"He's used to me singing in the car. Do you mind?" Again not waiting for an answer she began… "How much is that doggie in the window?"

Two choruses and four sneezes later Ben surprisingly found himself singing along. Well, you know how the saying goes and he felt completely beaten at this moment.

This had been a Play Group song. He recalled that there were accompanying actions then but today he'd leave that area to the resources of the canine section now playing a full part in the rear of the vehicle.

He had to admit he was beginning to enjoy the company of this mad female despite his allergy problem.

He turned towards her.

"Think I'd make it on X Factor?" and, totally out of character, he added, "we could try to form a duo."

"Or even a trio." She glanced round and Ben in response, hairy Ben that is, leaned his head forward and licked her neck. Taxi driver Ben had a sudden feeling of jealousy at their nearness but this was just as quickly dispelled by a movement behind and what felt like an early bath! Perhaps not!

They were nearing the village.

"You still haven't found out how she came to be in the road." Somehow it didn't seem important any more.

"If you could pull into the car park, that'll be fine. We're late so I'll have to rush."

Then with the car at a standstill, "Thanks for the lift. See you around some time perhaps."

And with that she was out accompanied by one very bouncy Ben, while the other Ben seemed to have turned to stone.

He watched her disappear through the pub door… some sort of fancy dress party was the best he could come up with. It all seemed a bit of a dream.

"Are you just going to sit there?"

But before he could answer, Ben's musing was

suddenly cut short and his normal non-risk-taking nature rapidly returned, as, alongside him, the car door was pulled open and a hand placed on his arm.

"So glad you could come. Amanda said you were here. I'm her father," and, without a pause, "we're all ready if you'll just follow me."

God… the vicar!

What was going on? What were they ready for? What was he supposed to be doing?

He would have expected to attend the midnight service tomorrow as usual with the family but a personal meeting with the vicar was definitely not in the plan.

He slid meekly out of the car, locked the door and followed towards the entrance.

Where was the lady in red? What he wanted to say to her at this moment was certainly not a blessing!

Into the lounge which attempted to give a warm welcome.

He glanced around.

Escape into the Gents… collapse in a heap… turn and make a run for it?

The all too silent vicar exerted control.

Ben resorted to silent prayer, "Help!"

On reaching the door at the far side, his companion stepped forward and, with a flamboyant gesture, opened it and ushered Ben forwards.

A deep intake of breath and Ben crossed the threshold to be greeted by a sea of smiling faces that erupted into the well known strains of "Happy Birthday to You."

So that was it…a carefully contrived way to get him to a surprise birthday party… the details of which an accomplished drama student, now dressed in a rather seductive little black number, tried to relate when they found themselves with a quiet moment together. She was failing dismally as Ben wasn't interested in what had happened three or four hours earlier. The holiday was starting on a high and the days ahead looked very promising. The surprise element of Christmas had returned.

And the Name is "Smith"

Just who was this man who was helping him paint the outside of the house? And even more how did the two of them fit together? Tom recalled Daphne's comment, "D'you think it's their real name?"

And then, "P'raps they're not even married."

Quickly followed by, "Not that it's any of our business!"

Tom would have been in full agreement.

Certainly, none of his business. Not until today, that is!

But for Daphne the speculation had started from the moment Mr and Mrs Smith arrived.

It had been Daphne's idea to move down to the coast and start running a Guest House.

Daphne was, always had been, and always would be, interested in people.

Tom accepted that this would be a new way of fulfilling her need to be around people.

He had to admit that Daphne was just the right sort of person to ensure a warm and friendly welcome for those choosing a holiday in South Devon.

Another major consideration for Tom had been his complete confidence in his wife's ability to cope with all paperwork involved.

Now, nearly three years later, Tom felt able to say that it had proved a good move.

The increased journey distance to work had proved hardly noticeable and calls to assist with D.I.Y. jobs had shown no significant increase.

The woodshed and the golf course provided, when required, space to get away.

Yes. Everything had worked out fine.

In fact nothing had really changed for him.

Daphne seemed to love every minute of it. And so did the visitors judging from repeat bookings!

An unwritten rule in B&B establishments that, provided payment is settled and behaviour is reasonable, no questions should be asked, had never needed to be faced.

Daphne heard it all.

And Tom had the rehashed version over their evening meal.

Family circumstances… Health conditions… Previous holiday disasters.

Tom heard the lot, occasionally accompanied by the odd item of photographic evidence.

The visitors provided readymade fuel for Daphne's lively imagination.

Tom knew only too well how Daphne's thoughts could catch fire.

He had quickly discovered a technique of half

listening in the quiet confidence that no inspired response was required.

That was until today.

Mr and Mrs Smith arrived on 3rd August and gave a London address.

They booked in for two weeks, paid cash and said nothing!

They rapidly became Daphne's personal challenge, and she reported back to Tom each evening.

While serving breakfast, Daphne was able to confirm her first impression that they were forty-ish.

"His hair is definitely receding and she will need to do something about the grey soon."

"They're both wearing wedding rings, not that that means anything these days."

"D'you think they're teachers wanting to get away from it all?"

It seemed to fit. But surely there was no pressing need to get away from each other and yet they seldom went out together.

"Mr went swimming today. I think he went to the Sports Centre. He hung his towel on the line."

On the third time of hearing that Mrs had gone out immediately after breakfast, Tom began to wish that the 'No Vacancies' had been in place on Monday.

"He went on a Creek Cruise today." Saturday bulletin, when Tom got back from a round of golf.

"I recognised his silly cap!"

"And, would you believe it? She arrives back in a car at lunch time, just popped in and then off she went again."

"I don't think it was the same car as last time," she added. "D'you think one of them is someone famous?"

Just fancy a famous film star or TV personality choosing to stay at 'The Horizon!'

Daphne tried to look closely as she served their Full English Breakfast.

Was it him or her?

She observed that neither of them seemed particularly worried about cholesterol. She was sure that famous people usually were.

"They don't dress right either!" she informed Tom.

Failed again.

On Tuesday evening Tom realised, too late, that he had set things well and truly alight.

Prompted by what he was reading in the evening paper, it just slipped out.

"Perhaps your Mr and Mrs Smith are planning some criminal activity!"

Daphne's mind had run riot!

It all seemed so ridiculous now after sharing a paint pot with a thoroughly nice guy who had halved his painting time.

But did he know where his wife, if it was his wife, had spent the day?

Tom had taken Thursday off.

He intended to paint the pebbledash rendering on the outside of the house over the weekend. Daphne had decided that light blue might be more in keeping with the building.

After the last two days Tom was in need of time to himself and a round of golf would provide that.

He decided on a leisurely lunch in the clubhouse before beginning painting early afternoon.

It was as he was sitting relaxing in the bar that he saw her.

"There she was, seated in the far window alcove, in the company of three men. None of whom," he added with great relish, "was our Mr Smith!"

Daphne, returned from an afternoon shopping, had hardly been given chance to comment on Tom's handiwork, before finding herself in this role reversal situation.

She sat with riveted attention.

"And more to the point," Tom continued, "one of them was Clive Partridge, Senior Partner of Partridge and Long! I didn't recognise the others but, whatever was going on, they were having quite a discussion and obviously enjoying each other's company. I made sure she didn't see me. I left by the side door. Anyway they were far too involved with each other to notice me."

A quick intake of breath.

"And then I get back here and he spends all the afternoon helping me while she's out living it up!"

Daphne had never heard Tom quite so animated before.

She didn't know what to think.

Could there really be something sinister going on?

"D'you know if she's back yet?"

"I haven't seen her."

And, as if on cue, a gentle knock on their door.

Picture Mrs Smith clutching a large bunch of garden flowers, not a bouquet, just ordinary mixed garden flowers.

"I wonder if you have a vase I could borrow until Monday. I would so like to take these home."

Having found something suitable, Daphne decided there was no way she could contemplate the request as coming from a hardened criminal!

It was only later in the evening that Tom remembered to tell Daphne that the Smiths were sleeping away that night and so would not require Sunday breakfast.

Well they were supposedly together.

They had paid in advance so if they didn't come back, well they didn't come back!

"And I get the flowers!" said Daphne.

The taxi came for the Smiths at 10.30 on Monday morning.

As they were leaving, Daphne's friend, June, arrived for coffee.

From the window, Daphne was surprised to see the three in conversation.

"I didn't know our new curate was staying with you," June said, as she sank down in the easy chair.

And before Daphne could confess that she didn't know anything about Mr Smith, "She and her husband are moving down from London at the end of the month. Such a good idea to come and get a feel of the place don't you think?"

Tulips from Amsterdam

"What about Molly who lists her interests as shopping, TV and gardening?"

A good number… well about fifteen… had come along to try to get the togetherness idea from the local comprehensive off the ground.

Mary glanced round. She smiled. No doubt that they all fitted comfortably into the upper age bracket… the vicar himself wasn't far off… and they were all, on occasions, guilty of generalising about young people.

"Help bridge the age gap," the letter had said.

They'd all responded positively when the vicar read it out last week, but it would take a mighty long bridge to span some of the chasms already mentioned.

Molly… shopping, TV and gardening.

None of the previously mentioned interests had even hinted at anything that even loosely came within her range. What did she have in common with discos, makeup or boys, all of which seemed to figure most prominently? But gardening…yes there was a link, a possibility, and before she knew what had happened, she was on her feet.

"Molly sounds like the one for me." The words were out.

A delighted Revd Hayward placed her name on the list, alongside Molly Evans, and the link was established.

All this had taken place some time ago and she was now awaiting Molly's fourth visit.

Where was she? Timekeeping was important. Being late actually bordered on rudeness.

Perhaps she wouldn't bother to come. Perhaps she'd been struck down by the flu or something. Both seemed unlikely, as Molly had appeared healthy and keen. To even harbour such thoughts seemed uncharitable. She knew some of the other pairings had failed but everything had been going well and she'd begun to hope that Molly might stay…

With advancing years life was beginning to centre on memories. She'd seen it happen in others and vowed it wouldn't happen to her but somehow it just crept up. Molly presented a lifeline… she so wanted her to come.

Molly was actually sitting, very uncomfortably, on a Number 39 bus. The bus was also sitting, waiting for an opportunity to move forward once the way ahead was clear.

The reason for Molly's discomfort was that there was not enough room on the seat for her, her backpack, and the lady with the basket. The bus was crowded. Almost all the seats were taken when she got on and she had just managed to squeeze on the edge.

Now she was going to be late. She knew Miss

Tunstall would not be pleased. Miss Tunstall didn't like people being late. Molly couldn't imagine she had ever liked people being late. She was sure that, despite her size, everyone would have recognised Miss Tunstall as someone you didn't mess with. Nobody would have risked being late for their shift at the hospital. Molly smiled. Her Mum and the other women at the factory never bothered about timekeeping. Mr Potts had no control. Things would be different if Miss Tunstall took over as foreman. Molly loved her Mum but she so wished she was more interested in her. She never listened to anything she said. She'd tried to tell her about volunteering for the 'age gap thing.' She always seemed too tired to bother about what was happening. She had to face it… her Mum just didn't care! But Miss Tunstall was different. Molly smiled but the smile faded as she pictured the tiny woman who would, by now, be feeling very irritated by her non arrival. Miss Tunstall was quite old… sixty-ish, or maybe even seventy. It was hard to tell because she was so lively. Her hair was grey, always neat and tidy. Miss Tunstall was a tidy person. So unlike herself!

Miss Tunstall hadn't commented on her size. Well she wouldn't, would she?

She was much too polite. But she must have noticed. Everyone else did.

The bus was moving.

This was her fourth visit. It was… the bus jerked to a stop again. Molly clutched at her small handbag to avoid it falling off her lap. Last week Miss Tunstall had mentioned tulips and in her bag she had a surprise. She so hoped Miss Tunstall would like it. On Saturday she'd searched all along the seed packets carefully lined up in the display at Homebase but she hadn't found one showing a picture of tulips. The painting of tulips hanging in Miss Tunstall's hallway was so bright. She'd liked it instantly. Miss Tunstall had said tulips were her favourite flower… something about seeing them growing in a special place years ago. And she liked Miss Tunstall. She'd had the idea about buying the seeds. She hoped that Miss Tunstall might want her to continue her visits as they began to grow. But the plan hadn't worked. She hadn't been able to find the right seeds but she'd found something else. Her hands closed tightly round the denim bag.

"Please, please, let her like it!"

9.25. Where was the girl? She didn't have that far to come. Bussing no doubt.

In her day she would have thought nothing of walking twice that distance. No wonder she was so overweight! No that was unkind… there might be some other reason. But she made her feel so small. Fourteen… how much more was she going to grow? She said she was going to bring a photo of her mother… perhaps it was a genes thing.

Interested in gardening. She'd only put that because she couldn't think of anything else… or so she said. She believed her actually because Molly was… well, to be believed. Their first meeting had been very difficult. To get the girl to speak at all had been like getting blood out of a stone, to use a cliché. But Molly is not cliché material. On the second visit she had opened up and shared so much. It had been quite embarrassing to hear

Molly talking so calmly about things she herself would never dream of mentioning. Molly must have been completely shell shocked on that first visit with everything so different. You had to hand it to the girl. It must have taken a great deal of courage to actually come up to the door, even though they had already met at the school's open evening.

But today she was late. Perhaps she really wasn't going to come. Had it been acting when she had seemed really interested as they'd talked about seeds in the garden? She'd had a go with the pruning. It had needed to be explained several times and it was unlikely that she would remember the word secateurs but she'd done well. Molly had said her Mum wouldn't have had such patience. Patience. Mary shivered as her thoughts flew to… the ward… the incident. How many times had she relived that day? Rules were rules… there for a reason… not to be broken… but at any cost? The tears almost unheeded at the time now pricked the back of her eyes. Where was she now? Had she alone been instrumental in the loss of a good nurse? She'd learned so much since her time on the wards, the book of life they called it, but the 'if only' thoughts never fully went away. She had begun to hope that Molly might help to heal the wound.

The sound of the doorbell brought her back into the present. It rang again as she made her way into the hallway. Expectation soared. She was sure it could only be Molly.

From the moment there was the slightest gap between door and frame, Mary was bombarded by words; apologies, explanation, the bus, the traffic, sorry!

Silence only came when, with door fully open, a rather crumpled paper bag was thrust towards her.

"I do hope you like it." Then more words fell out. "It wasn't what I wanted. I was looking for seeds but I couldn't find the right ones. Go on. Open it!"

Eyes full of anticipation seemed to fill the whole face of a highly animated Molly who was, incidentally, still on the wrong side of the doorstep.

Mary carefully removed the simple wrapping and her tiny hands responded with what might be described as reverence to the article entrusted to them.

Printed across the bright flowers she read, "A present from Amsterdam."

Molly moved forward and they were both in the hallway.

"Do you like it? I saw it in a charity shop and I know how much you like tulips. Please say you like it!"

Mary Tunstall took a deep breath and allowed herself just one glance up at her picture before focussing on Molly.

"It's lovely. Really lovely. But far too nice to drink from. Thank you very much Molly."

A pause… and then emotionally in charge once more,

"I've got some things planned for us to do today but let's get inside first and catch up on news."

Tulip seeds! Whatever next?

She made a mental note that in the autumn she'd introduce Molly to tulip bulbs and then they could enjoy planting them together.

The Seagull

So this was it. The 'what had to be done' of the last few days was accomplished, and Margaret could no longer hide in busyness. As if someone flicked the switch to set her feet in motion, she followed the black coated figure and took up her indicated position in the front row. She forced herself to look up and her emotions were instantly thrown into turmoil as she faced… the seagull!

Margaret hated it! It was so ridiculous. She knew her mother couldn't bear birds being near her for the majority of her life and yet, on this day of all days, she, an only daughter, had to sit here and look at a seagull perched on her mother's coffin. There should have been a beautiful family wreath but, instead, there was a bird standing there.

What would everybody think?

The close family had known about this late request added to her mother's funeral wishes. They, of course, also knew the reason behind it. No doubt some others, having got over their initial surprise, would put two and two together, but the majority of those who had gathered to 'Farewell' Emily, would be amazed to find themselves looking at a floral tribute in the form of a seagull.

"We are gathered here today…"

The place was full. As she glanced sideways, Margaret

could see that some people were standing around the doorway as well as those along the side. There was no doubt that her mother was well loved. If only she could concentrate on what was being said. She had been dreading how she would cope with this day and yet now her thoughts and attention seemed to be trapped by the magnetic power of this wretched bird.

She was glad that Fiona had come with her to see Natasha. Fiona had always been very close to her grandmother and had been a great support with all the arrangements. Well, all the family had been supportive but Fiona had sort of taken charge of the planning.

"A seagull out of flowers."

The surprise had been clear but how quickly Natasha had regained her composure after the initial shock. No, she'd never done anything quite like that, but Emily and Fred had been very special customers from the day when she'd provided flowers for their wedding twenty years earlier. She would be very pleased to fulfil this last request for Emily.

It was a tribute to her outstanding floristry skills that the assembled company felt as if they were sharing the occasion with a real bird. The clearly stated instruction that it must look towards the rear of the coffin meant there was eye-to-eye contact which made it even more of a horror situation for Margaret. Whatever was her mother thinking of?

"Each little flower that opens, each little bird that sings"
Margaret was conscious of the younger grandchildren singing the words, as well known now as when she

had been a child, but one would be severely stretched to describe the sound made by gulls as singing. She knew her mother had chosen this hymn with her great-grandchildren in mind. The older ones had come to Grandpa Fred's funeral. It had been such a sad affair with lots of tears. She hadn't wanted a repeat of that at her own funeral.

With Fred gone, and on her own again, Emily had sunk into great sadness. Her sparkle seemed to have evaporated. There had been questions around her remarrying in her late sixties, all completely unfounded as it had turned out, but there had been even greater concern as to whether, in her late eighties, on her own again, there would be any restoration of purpose and enjoyment in life. The home, which everyone liked to visit with its nearness to the sea, felt bereft and lonely.

"Some of you who have known Emily for a long time will recall her determination in coping as a young widow with a baby and then rejoiced as she found happiness comparatively late in life in her marriage to Fred."

Margaret was aware that details of her mother's life were being celebrated around her as stories were shared with the gathered company: the teenager who insisted on gaining a bookkeeping qualification when her father wanted her to just stay at home, a move that not only provided a means of employment but also meant that the church was treated to the pristine pages of accounts from the hand of their long-serving treasurer: members of the youth club, now bringing up families of their own, who would always remember the smile which greeted them from behind the refreshment counter: the windswept figure rattling a collection tin in support of her boss's favourite charity… then the totally unexpected discovery of a new loving relationship. A ripple of laughter greeted the reference to Graham having given away his mother-in-law, but Margaret silently remembered the moment when a small hand extended sideways grasped hers as the emotion of the moment threatened to prove too much for her mother. So many had gathered to celebrate that April day. How quickly Emily and Fred had settled into their new home and become part of the community around the court.

So many people now had sent cards of sympathy. Margaret intended to read all the messages properly later but the overwhelming sentiment was that "everyone loved her mother."

For no apparent reason, a sharp feeling of guilt suddenly hit her… her mother's love for her was never in doubt but had she really loved her mother?

The family had decided to purchase a seat in memory of Fred. It seemed a good idea and had actually proved to be an inspiration. The seat was situated overlooking the busy harbour entrance and despite her mother's decreased mobility it was within easy walking distance from the court. The elderly couple had so enjoyed their walks near the sea. The seat would provide a focal point for the family in their remembrance, but nobody could have foreseen the revolution it brought to Emily's life.

Margaret recalled the phone call from her mother's next-door neighbours. The excitement in Peggy's voice was enough to confirm that something good had happened, something special for their dear friend Emily. A miracle they called it.

Apparently, on one of her visits to the seat Emily had re-encountered Fred. Fred the man, that is, reincarnated in the form of Fred the seagull. A herring gull to be precise. Emily needed to get it right. With his knowledge of birds, Fred would want that.

Emily's complete revitalisation had occurred. Weather permitting there followed daily visits to the seat for her meeting with Fred. Amongst other things, Fred was treated to his favourite biscuits and cheese, wholemeal bread and freshly cut apple. The fact that there were always other gulls around didn't seem to bother Emily. She had rediscovered the love of life.

Margaret had failed dismally when questioned by her granddaughter Tracey about reincarnation. Later she had overheard Tracey and Alex discussing the matter. Cousins were often more useful in sharing ideas than grandparents who seldom felt confident to give any answers. No doubt these young people would learn one day that life actually got more complicated the older you got. All Margaret knew was that her mother had found a new lease of life. She had secretly watched her on one occasion, seated patiently waiting. She listened to the cry of the gulls as they wheeled overhead, birds and water in the freedom of close harmony… a sound condemned as so out of place in the city centre. She'd watched as one bird landed on the rail in front of her mother, clumsily moved to the arm of the seat, snatched something from the pile of goodies, then up and away pursued by its screaming compatriots. And her mother actually believed that was Fred.

"In John's Gospel we read: In my Father's house are many rooms. I go to prepare a place for you..."

God, that bird's got such a cruel looking beak.

Could what she had done be described as cruelty?

Margaret knew the neighbours had thought so at the time.

The small stroke, the increased loss of memory, the need for twenty four hour care, there had been no other choice but Heather House.

Was that the right thing to do?

Some people thought she should have had her mother to live with her but they both knew that wouldn't have worked. Those who had witnessed Emily's new lease of life certainly equated removing her from the seat and Fred was tantamount to cruelty.

But then they hadn't reckoned that the same God, who some would blame for the health blow, had yet more surprises in store.

Margaret wondered how Carol and the other members of staff, who had managed to come, were feeling at this moment... genuine sadness accompanied, if they were honest, by a sense of relief she suspected. The problem of Emily, the patio and the birds had been solved for them. It was ironic that the separation of Emily and her seagull had been seen as a problem for everyone except Emily herself. Hadn't Fred's father kept homing pigeons? So, of course, Fred would know where to find her. They all loved Emily to bits and they had gone along with the story. Most of the staff admitted to secretly observing this little old lady seated talking to an audience of fluttering pigeons while waiting for a passing gull... Fred... to risk a downwards swoop to snatch up one of the tasty morsels before wheeling back into the open sky with a cry of thanks. Here, land invading gulls, birds considered by most as a wretched nuisance, caused many a smile. Carol had done everything she could to put off the evil day when she would have to tell Emily that the management could no longer tolerate the health hazard of the birds on the patio. Now the problem had been solved for her. It was just typical of Emily's whole life spent in caring about others that things should have turned out this way.

"The Lord is my shepherd. I'll not want. We will sing those wonderful words of comfort taken from the 23rd Psalm. And then will you please remain standing for the committal."

Heavens! It was almost the end. Margaret was conscious of rising to her feet as the gentle organ music filled the room.

A shaft of sunlight caught the side of the coffin and the bird's wing nearest the window and gradually spread out forming a circle of light.

Margaret gazed at the transformation of beauty in front of her. The well known words came from all around, passed Margaret and surrounded wood and bird in an aura of peace.

And in a moment, Margaret realised what her mother had done for her in death as well as life… how could she describe it? Yes. Together they shared a peace beyond understanding.

The mechanics of the next few minutes passed without any physical involvement on her part.

It was completed.

As her legs mechanically propelled her out of the building Margaret was conscious of a small hand gripping hers.

"Hurry up Grandma! We must get outside to see Great Gran fly away with Grandpa Fred, just like on your willow-pattern plate."

And that was the moment when the tears broke through.

The Surprise Package

Daniel was feeling very sorry for himself as he walked home from work.

Yesterday's plans had all gone awry. Late night shopping held little attraction now after the disaster of last night. Somehow he had to get his mind away from it. He had completely lost all evidence of the 'feel-good' factor of life.

How had things gone so wrong? Perhaps he should just keep away from women for a while. But Joanne wasn't just another woman, she was, and still is, if he was honest…different.

He crossed the bridge glancing down into the dark waters below. No, it wasn't quite that bad but nevertheless he shivered as black thoughts tried to take over. He walked round towards the railway station. Already there seemed plenty of people starting off towards Christmas gatherings. The students had departed long ago and with them the long queues for buses up the hill.

What should he do about Joanne? They'd been getting on so well. The thought of spending Christmas in the flat on his own sent his spirits descending still further.

Deep in thought, he was passing the police station when a young female officer came out and, taking him firmly by the arm, said, "We need your help."

In a moment Daniel found himself propelled through the swing doors and into the station foyer.

"Sorry about this," she smiled, "thing is we're desperate to carry out an identity parade and we need one more male your sort of height and age." She paused. "Have you ever done this before?"

A couple of years ago Daniel had taken part in a line up but that had happened in a much more controlled way. Even then he had found the experience quite daunting, not being able to see the witness who was giving you the 'once over' was bad enough but what if he'd been picked out. Of course he wasn't and he'd survived. He'd almost forgotten the whole incident… until now that is.

A faltering "Yes," somehow got out of his mouth and before he could add any "buts…

"Well that's fine then. It really is good of you to help us in this way, what with Christmas so near and all."

If he'd been dealing with a male officer Daniel thought he might have been able to protest but somehow this female never allowed you to think anything other than that she was in charge. He meekly followed her through the door, down the corridor and then into a small room.

"Just one more thing, would you please put on this Father Christmas outfit. The boots fit all sizes and the beard is fixed via the adhesive on the table."

This couldn't be happening! He must be dreaming. But the W.P.C. whoever she was, just stood there as if she'd made an everyday request.

A few minutes later, coat, boots and beard in place… he supposed he looked OK as there wasn't a mirror in the room… Daniel obediently followed along behind the law. He was ushered through a door at the end of the corridor to join… so he wasn't the only mad fool… a line of similarly clad figures.

"Decide where you want to stand." He responded like a lamb.

"Gentlemen, please pick up the card in front of you and display the number towards the front."

Was she officious! She reminded him of Anne Robinson on The Weakest Link… at least he didn't have to answer any questions.

"The witness will be passing along the line behind the glass. She can see you but you can't see her. Any clear identification will then be addressed."

So it was another 'she.' Daniel found himself wondering what the new 'she' looked like. Why on earth was she trying to pick out a Father Christmas?

Will the real Father Christmas please stand up! He smiled inwardly. At this moment he wasn't enjoying standing up, he wished he'd had chance to go for a wee, no doubt it was just an imagined reaction to the situation. He just had to patiently stand and wait.

And then it was over.

"Thank you, gentlemen. You are free to go… except number six."

Daniel turned to follow the line and then… No! It couldn't be true! He was Number six!

A hand on his arm, along another passage, down some steps and into, clearly displayed for all to see, Cell Three.

"Someone will be with you in a moment to settle your affairs," and the door was closed with considerable force. In a state of shock, Daniel hadn't even been aware that the owner of the arm on this occasion was a male officer.

Father Christmas in a cell... what a picture!

This only happened in books or on the telly. He had no idea even of what he was supposed to have done.

He sank down on the bench.

A day in the life of Daniel Palmer... heaven knows what the next day might bring.

It was all too bizarre... almost laughable really.

Reality surfaced. Never mind tomorrow, how about the next few hours?

The sound of a key in the door caused him to raise his head from his hands.

"Daniel."

"Joanne!"

He was stunned. The very last person he would have ever expected to see. What the...?

And then suddenly reason returned. He was Father Christmas and yet...

"How come you recognised me beneath all this gear?"

She was down beside him and, and burying her head in his beard, explained how she'd wanted to find a way to say, "Sorry," and how she had a cousin who was in the police force, and how it was nearly Christmas and...

Daniel wasn't really listening. How could he be angry with such a woman? Hadn't he said all along that this one was something special?

As he started to rather gingerly remove the hairiness

which was definitely obstructing closeness, he was aware of something that was bugging him.

Even Wonder Woman must have limits. He confronted her.

"How come you persuaded those other nine guys to be part of your devious plan?"

"Easy. They're actually the members of the police choir and they're singing in the precinct tonight." And then, with the most arresting of smiles, she added, "I thought you might like to join them!"

"Hark, the herald angels sing."

Daniel, no longer dressed in red, squeezed Joanne's hand as, along with other shoppers they joined in the singing. As a child Daniel had loved the element of surprise in Christmas. He smiled. He'd certainly had his share today. Only three hours ago who'd have thought… He placed an arm around the surprise package beside him. It might only be 22nd December but, for him, Christmas had definitely come early this year.

A Heavy Load

I was aware of him from some distance. Why? I suppose it was because he made me feel uneasy.

The problem of homelessness was increasing. I had been accosted several times recently. It wasn't the choice language or fear of violence, not even the occasional accompanying skinny dog that perturbed me; it was just trying to cope with ignoring the request for help. I knew where the money would probably go but the same Bible words always rang in my ears making me feel very uncomfortable.

If I crossed over the road I wouldn't have to face the problem!

Get a grip on yourself woman! You know what you decided.

Two people passed me and I noted that the crouching figure had made no attempt to approach them. He just sat there surrounded by the carrier bags… one man… so many bags.

"Carrying her home in two carrier bags." The line from the wellknown song hummed its way into my mind. This man certainly had far more possessions than that. However many bags were there?

He was wearing a combat jacket. He seemed intent on studying the pavement, preventing any clear look at his face. My immediate impression suggested hair rather shorter and tidier than I would have expected.

As I approached, he moved. With great care he inserted his fingers through the handles of the bags... three, no four on each side... locked thumbs into clenched fists, and, slowly uncoiling his back lifted.

He struggled to stand up. He was not as young as I had imagined and he was definitely not as strong as he would have liked to be! What on earth was in those bags? From previous casual observation this kind of bag usually contained all sorts of bits and pieces of... well... rubbish, none of which would cause a weighing scales much problem. But here was something else.

He was on the move... slowly. I was past and rapidly moving out of his life, leaving behind an encounter that might be set on back burner for future anecdotal use. There had been no opportunity for any meeting of our eyes and I was congratulating myself on the way my conscience had managed to cope, when it happened. The sound was loud enough to cause me to instantly wheel round. The picture confronting me made me want to laugh and cry at the same time.

Tins! Tins rolling in all directions. Most tins were rolling while a few just sat.

One mystery was solved. The contents of the bags, or at least a large percentage of them, lay open to all.

And there, in the middle of the confusion, their owner, apparently turned to stone, standing, head in hands, in an 'I need help,' sort of pose.

How is it that everybody, or almost everybody, vanishes on this sort of occasion?

The 'all' previously mentioned observers consisted of two young boys, an elderly couple walking on the other side of the road and me.

My inner self took over.

I had strength I could move. And I had a large, almost empty, sport's bag.

"Need a hand?"

No response. So I just got on with it.

"Bags aren't nearly so strong these days."

A quick glance indicated just three bags, plus contents remained intact.

The two boys, having retrieved a few tins from the gutter, ran off laughing.

Gradually the errant tins found a more secure resting place alongside my swimming gear. The labels declared that 'Economy' was the name of the game! Here was a customer who clearly believed in making the most of his money! Having witnessed his earlier struggle, I knew that there was no way he could lift this one considerably heavier load.

I placed a hand on his arm.

The touch proved to be an awakening.

The statue came to life… to a highly agitated state of life… and his tongue took over.

The words poured out in a completely disjointed fashion, moving through the subjects of tins, the supermarket, home, time, his mother, hunger, the house, all muddled together, round and back again, never finishing anything as he tried to cope with the situation.

"Do you live far away?" I forced my way into the jumble.

The panic stopped abruptly, and, with an accompanying hand gesture, he answered perfectly clearly.

"Just round the corner behind the flats."

"I'll help you then. You take those two," I indicated two carrier bags, "and," as I picked up the sport's bag, hastily pushing in the last carrier, "I'll bring this."

He tried to protest about my carrying such a large bag. I stood my ground.

He seemed to accept that I was in charge and gave in. I followed towards the flats.

As we walked I had time to wonder what 'home' would be like. The quick response to my question certainly affirmed that this man did indeed have a home, not quite what I had first surmised. He stepped out quite confidently, no problem with walking. I could now see trousers and shoes clearly and these also went contrary to my 'first sight' assumption. Perhaps I had got it all wrong and he was just, well, sort of mentally mixed up or whatever you call it. You know, one of the 'being cared for in the community' statistics.

We rounded the flats, and there in front of me was a row of small terraced houses, no front gardens, and doors opening straight on to the pavement sort of closeness.

"I've lived here all my life. He turned and spoke to me as we stopped outside Number Four.

"When my mother died, the council let me stay on." He fumbled in his pocket, found the key, and, as he fitted it in the lock, added, "Watch out you don't fall over the boxes. The passage is quite dark even at this time of day."

I braced myself for what might be revealed. First bags. Now boxes!

I stepped gingerly through the open door and was greeted by two walls of boxes, one on either side. Double stacked, they provided a sort of guard of honour as we moved into a small sitting room. I was so glad that my large bag arrived safely without causing any demolition act *en route*.

He indicated a chair and I sank into it thankfully. I was glad my efforts had generated a bit of a sweat as there appeared to be no heat in this house.

I viewed my surroundings.

My eyes slowly took in the immaculate little room. I felt transported back in time… the only present day intrusion being yet more boxes squeezed into available spaces between furniture.

My gaze drawn to the mantelpiece moved along the line of photographs and returned to the central, silver-framed print.

He must have been watching.

"That's my Mum and Dad on their wedding day," he said. "I never knew Dad. He was killed before I was born. Mum used to say I looked like him." He made it all sound so matter of fact. He spoke with such pride and no sign of anger or distress.

In contrast, I was speechless. Only half an hour ago I was just following my normal Wednesday routine… what had I got myself into?

From the safety of my chair, things were becoming clearer.

Here was a man, forced to cope on his own, so intent on making sure he never went hungry, that he felt compelled to keep a food store… and, somehow, it had all got out of hand.

I wouldn't be surprised if there were boxes of food elsewhere in the house.

I smiled at the thought that hopefully he had more than one tin opener, just in case!

"Is there an empty box for today's tins?" I was more than able to join in the game.

"Just put them there by the settee," he said, "I can deal with them later. I don't want to delay you you've been so kind."

I started removing the tins and it was only then that I noticed today everything he had purchased was soup: tomato, vegetable, oxtail, but all soup. He obviously was a little unbalanced. It would take ages for one man to consume so much soup.

"You must be wondering about the soup."

The voice commanded that I should look up. Our eyes met for the first time.

"This place is a depot for the Soup Run for people on the streets. They needed storage and I don't need all this space for myself. Someone comes to bring new stuff or collect as required."

He was laughing now.

"That episode this morning was due to a generous donation and my failure to realise how far the money would go… or how heavy tins are! But it's all turned out all right, thanks to your kindness."

The morning's happenings went through several reruns as I swam up and down the pool. I kicked hard to try to get the guilt feeling out of my system.

"Will Alison please come to reception."

A loudspeaker staff call, as I left the pool, provided me with a final sobering thought.

"And I never even asked his name!"

Pen Friends

"How are you getting on with it?"

I glanced up as the voice came from above.

"The book. How do you like it?"

"Oh, the book." (Deep breath Alison, regain composure.)

The book was my security. It was residing towards the edge of the table alongside a bowl of fresh fruit I'd collected from the buffet bar. Eating on your own is bad enough at any time, but, in another country for the first time, I definitely needed something to hide behind.

"It's fine." (What did that mean?) "I only started it last night and I'm about halfway through." (Indicated clearly, I noticed, by the protruding Jane Austen bookmark.)

The conference had finished early so I had enjoyed the luxury of a whole evening reading.

"It's not what I thought."

(Control Alison. Don't panic.)

I looked at the voice for the first time as it continued.

"Sorry I thought it was the one based in Singapore."

I've heard of opening gambits… was this American style?

"The setting for this one is Egypt," (hand placed on book) "Nasser and Farouk and all that. It's quite clever really, the way fiction is woven around facts."

That should floor him! Yes, he looked abashed. Nice eyes though.

I took a sip of coffee as if he wasn't there.

"Well, must dash. Might see you around later."

I inhaled and then exhaled forcibly, a 'space invaded' sort of gesture. Now perhaps I could continue my breakfast in peace.

There are certain musts when spending a day by the pool in Sunnyvale. With only one return visit to the apartment I had the lot, plus the bonus of nobody else around.

I arranged myself between a lounger and a parasol table

I had a dual purpose in staying these two extra days, the main being to relax and enjoy the Californian sunshine, with the secondary aim of completing the story. Having decided to have a go at the competition, discipline had proved sadly lacking. There was no excuse now! I had a clear strategy… read one chapter on the lounger and then some writing.

The day progressed well.

As I emerged from one of the regular cooling off sessions in the pool that I heard the voice again.

"Mind if I join you?"

The American was back. He seemed even taller. I felt self-conscious as I noted his sun tan. I clutched the towel closer. Nice smile.

He was actually moving a lounger so my answer seemed of little consequence.

"You're a writer." He was now standing next to the table which was littered with pieces of paper.

"Not really. It's just a competition I'm having a go at. I doubt if I'll even finish it… actually I work for a travel agent. (Just keep waffling Alison to gain time to gather up the evidence and avoid the embarrassment of his reading anything.)

"Where are you based in the U.K.?"

"Bath. Have you ever visited England?"

"Several times… never been to Bath but I'd certainly like to."

"You should… it rates second to London on the tourist map." (Suppose he came on business.)

I relaxed somewhat. I was on home ground and we chatted on about my city and the U.K. in general. He really was very easy to talk with…not a typical American male…correction… he didn't fit my definition!

"What are you doing for dinner tonight Alison?"

(Had I told him my name? Inner panic! Help!)

"How d'you fancy Japanese?"

The cheek of the man. I might have all sorts of plans… but I hadn't and a pizza in my apartment sounded a very weak excuse.

"Sounds fine. I love Chinese but I've never been to a Japanese restaurant."

"This place is considered as special even by U.S. standards, but we need to eat early.

"Seven o'clock O.K.?"

"Fine."

"By the way, the name's Bob."

I consciously spent longer than usual getting ready. Special attention to makeup especially my nose which seemed to have missed the sun cream. The mirror convinced me that the dress should be all right.

The evening was an experience!

A personal chef cooked everything on a hotplate at our table demonstrating considerable skill of knife juggling while his amazing mastery of language facilitated very lively comments that added to the occasion.

Bob was excellent company. He just exuded confidence and seemed to increase mine. I observed how good he looked whatever his mode of dress. The food was wonderful. I hadn't enjoyed an evening so much for ages.

All too soon we were driving back.

As we neared the motel I felt a sudden wave of apprehension. What now?

Bob chatted on about Anglo-American relationships and I agreed, wondering if we were talking about the same thing.

Fortunately we were.

In the morning he had gone. When I went into breakfast the receptionist handed me the note.

Alison. Thanks for the evening. Enjoy the rest of your stay Will keep in touch. Bob

Three weeks later the package arrived.

The American stamps must mean Bob, but why a package?

The package contained a book and another note.

From one writer to another! Hope you finished the story and that you will enjoy reading my latest about Singapore. See you in Bath sometime. Yours, Robert Sheldon"

The Rainbow-Coloured Scarf

(This story and the following poem are based on personal experience)

"So how are we going to celebrate Dad? I'm not expecting an answer but I wanted to ask you. There's lots of things I want to ask you."

Is this the right moment? Is there ever a right moment? If there is then surely this must be it.

"I'll make a decision and I promise to make it a celebration even if it is just you and me."

Let's begin at the beginning.

I don't know what life was like for you as a child…or life in general in 1908… I can check in history books but that doesn't tell me how it was for you. The birth of a son must have been a time for a real celebration… the chance to carry on the family name… follow in father's footsteps and all that. Hopes, plans, future thoughts… isn't that the same with the birth of any child? Place of birth, Portsmouth where I am headed. I wonder if somehow you managed to pass on a love of the place to me… don't think we could put it down to genes! Did you enjoy your childhood? I hope you weren't pressurised. I can imagine as an only one there could have been so much expectation placed on your shoulders. I wonder how often you walked along the seafront. I'm not going there today, of course, but I hope you know how I love doing just that. Come to think of it you couldn't have imagined that a daughter of yours, in the seventh decade of her life, would be part of a massed event along the seafront braving the worst of wind and rain. Smile about it Dad!

Were you well behaved at school? Don't suppose you had any option with threats of punishment hanging over you. You were obviously good at exams… is it a thing you like to remember or did you have the same feeling as me about not wanting to appear a swot in front of your friends? Come to think of it I wonder if you knew I felt like that. I was always reluctant to speak out about anything … I always wondered whether it was on account of family circumstances or might it have been an inherited characteristic?

I've always rated you pretty high Dad. I found it difficult to hear Mum talk of your short temper… something I'd never realised… perhaps I'd never allowed you to be fully human.

Now let's have a bit of honesty… were you disappointed I was a girl?

This is the gate. Actually the two large gates are fully opened extending a welcome to all visitors. My legs have suddenly decided they belong to someone else. I feel completely unable to move. Even the air around seems to have lost its breath.

"No!" A silent word of assertion. I am still in control.

This is the moment I have chosen and no matter how unusual I will ensure it remains a time of celebration.

Behind me the traffic continues transporting everyday people on everyday journeys completely unaware of me and their nearness to the focus of my day.

Composure regained I walk confidently between the iron structures, turn left and along the somewhat ill-kept path. No need for the tightly clutched instructions, I've rehearsed the route so many times in my mind. Turn right at the first junction then keep going until you meet the second cross path, then three in and…

I am gazing at my journey's end.

I read the well weathered inscription,

"Albert Bailey. Born 26th November 1908." No telegram from the Queen on this very special day. "Happy Birthday Dad."…My lips mouth the words as my eyes read on…

"Died 6th February 1939" … and the tears begin to flow.

So many emotions come pouring in as I stand at the graveside. Through my tears my eyes take in the vast space around… the stone memorials stretched in all directions but no other people about just like I'd hoped.

The suppressed anger of so many years bubbled up. "Why did you have to die so young Dad?"

Hell! It wasn't meant to be like this. What's happened to the celebration word?

My scarf takes over and carries out a mopping up job. As I try to smile again a strange thought takes over. A picture emerges of a huge company gathered here to celebrate with us. We are no longer alone. An uncanny feeling of warmth and wellbeing spreads through me.

I vaguely recall being brought here as a small child but necessity had taken Mum and me away from the city. Why had I waited so long to return? This seemed to be a moment for honesty.

"I only discovered when your birthday was Dad as we were sorted out our filing cabinet… important document section… I never gave it a thought before."

Was I looking for forgiveness at this late hour?

"Anyway, thanks for being my Dad even if we only had five months of life together."

After a moment's pause I added, "I wish it could have been longer," and no celebration or strength of dam could prevent the ensuing flood.

Suddenly the sound of cheering from the nearby football stadium carried on the wind broke into the situation.

The time for tears was over. I fastened my coat and retraced my steps. The celebration of life would continue for me.

I paused at the gateway and glanced back to where the company of dull grey stones was now punctuated by a spot of rainbow brightness.

Sometimes an emotional happening is best shared in poetic form. Hopefully the following poem will add something to my story.

The Man I Lived Without

I stand alone in company of many long since gone.

A cold wind murmurs in my ear
These weathered stones want you to hear
The might have been, the could have been,
The would have been, the should have been,
Futility of dreams.

A child's cry carried on the air,
Held high on shoulders of a handsome man,
Who keeps me safe, says, "Follow me,
My hope and joy, your destiny."
And yet I never knew him.

Fists clenched in anger stem a silent scream
As loneliness enfolds in chilling cloak.

Proud escort in the aisle of love,
A sideways glance, a proffered hand,
Assurance calms a moment's fear
Through bonded touch, paternal care,
It isn't fair…
A dulling greyness threatens power of thought
While sharpened knives pursue a breaking heart.

Another generation comes; new fatherhood is born
To walk together, talk together,
Run, play, live and laugh together,
One day die and be together,
Reality not fantasy, fuelling pangs of jealousy.

A passing gull invades with tuneless song
Mourning the tenderness for which I long.

Truncated trees cut off in prime of life
Wait leafless, trusting in new birth
As mists of time struggle to raise spirits
From remains encased in earth.
Unending contemplation… unexpected celebration
Humanity, eternity, a century in history.

Reach out and touch cold stone,
Trace name and numbers through the years and tears
And whisper, "Happy Birthday DAD."

Who's Afraid of the Big Bad Wolf?

The call had come to the office.

"Jan. I'm terribly sorry but you go on down. I'll be with you crack of dawn Sunday. You do understand don't you?"

I understood only too well that unexpected last minute meetings were always going to be a part of any relationship we shared.

A whole weekend together.

Where?

No problem.

Jeff's enthusiasm for Bath was obvious and I was only too glad to have the opportunity to check it out myself.

The ease of travel from London had, in the circumstances, proved a considerable bonus.

The soak in the warm, bubble filled, bath had almost completely removed any initial disappointment of arriving alone.

Lovely hotel, full of character as you walk through the door.

I hugged the towel round myself.

Mmm. It felt good and I felt good.

I walked over to the window and looked out.

And… there in the garden was a pig!

Country hotel. Pig in garden?.. Possibly.

In the centre of Bath? Very unlikely.

But… it was a pig… a large pig standing in the middle of the lawn.

And… it was not a sculpture!

As I dressed for supper my mind was filled with all sorts of ideas as to why the pig was there.

I went downstairs without an acceptable explanation.

The dining room was fairly full. Plenty of others making the most of the Bank Holiday break.

I hadn't eaten for some time and I was hungry.

I really enjoyed the meal. The service was excellent. Trust Jeff to get it right!

As I was leisurely drinking my coffee I considered asking if the pork was 'home grown!'

I couldn't stop thinking about that pig.

It was a lovely evening but I decided against a walk.

I left the dining room and went up in the lift.

I studied the leaflets I'd picked up in the foyer.

There wouldn't be any difficulty filling the time tomorrow.

A brief check of television programmes convinced me that an early night was the best idea.

Before getting into bed I just couldn't resist looking out at the garden.

The lawn was empty.

I woke up and it was still dark.

As usual it took a few moments to adjust to where I was.

And then I heard it… the sound of snoring.

Goodness! The walls in this place can't be very thick. Had I really been woken up by someone snoring?

There it was again.

Only…it sounded strange… not quite like proper snoring.

I concentrated.

And slowly it came to me.

The sound I had heard was the snorting of a pig… and the noise appeared to be coming from the bathroom.

A pig in my bathroom!

This couldn't be happening to me.

I curled up in bed with the duvet clasped under my chin. I was far too frightened to move. I lay there a long time after silence returned.

Eventually, I plucked up courage and switched on the light.

I was alone.

In the early morning everything seemed fine.

Perhaps it had all been a dream.

It had to be.

I showered, breakfasted, and was ready to go.

Saturday was mine to enjoy.

Bath lived up to its reputation and I didn't return to the hotel until almost five o'clock.

I'd had a lovely day.

I hoped Jeff would like the dress I'd bought. I just hadn't been able to resist it.

Swinging the carrier I almost skipped into the drive.

And... I froze!

Lying on the curve of the drive, pairs of teats fully displayed, was the most enormous sow!

Lying and waiting for what?

For me!

And while I gazed in disbelief several people walked past without apparently noticing the large animal.

I crossed to the other side of the drive and almost ran through the hotel door.

I had started up the stairs before I remembered I hadn't collected my key.

Compose yourself! There must be some explanation.

But why pigs? I must be going mad!

Still clutching my carrier, I gained the safety of my room and flung myself down on the bed.

I was shaking. Nothing like this had ever happened before. I wasn't going to move until tomorrow.

But how to survive the night?

The strident sound of the telephone made me jump.

I reached for the receiver.

"Jan. It's me."

"Jeff."

"I'm at the station. The meeting finished earlier

than expected so I'll be with you tonight. Train's in ten minutes. Everything OK?"

"Fine. Yes I'm fine."

"See you then. Love you."

"Love you too."

My night was transformed.

I showered and dressed with care and I became aware that I was humming.

The tune. "Who's Afraid of the Big Bad Wolf?"

The subconscious can play all sorts of tricks!

I smiled and decided not to mention the pigs to Jeff Well not today anyway.

Maintaining concentration during the walkabout guided tour the next day was proving quite a struggle.

Jeff had suggested it and I was only too ready to do anything as long we were together.

I clung on to his arm and went with the group.

The word Bladud caused a sudden rise in interest.

Our hotel was "The Bladud."

I gave our lady guide my full attention.

"Prince Bladud was cured of leprosy by our spa water. The healing power of the water was discovered, when a herd of pigs rolled in the swampy ground."

"Pigs!" The word hit me.

"Anyone seeing the ghost of a pig in Bath," she went on, "is assured of good luck for a whole year."

She smiled .

"That should make sure that you all join one of our renowned Ghost Walks!"

I gave Jeff's arm a squeeze.

"Who needs a Ghost Walk?"

"My good luck arrived on the 5.35 from Paddington."

No Future in the Past

"Now that's more like it!"

Stephanie had caught sight of a guy at the back of the group.

She had agreed to join in this Freshers' Week visit to Warwick Castle but in no way was she an historian. She was into the here and now. New acquaintance, Fiona, was part of the now.

She had very quickly discovered that Fiona was into history, which meant keeping within touching distance of the guide, 'Mavis the Voice,' as Stephanie had christened her, clearly did not come from the Midlands. Fine. Fiona could have Mavis while she checked out the talent in the group.

Not very inspiring… until now!

He was something else!

She wondered how it had taken her so long to notice him. He definitely hadn't travelled on their coach.

She could see his head and shoulders through a gap… very unusual haircut… seemed to suit his face though. If only he'd look her way.

She started to edge round.

They'd been up the wide staircase... done the picture gallery... and... well they'd gone up and still had to go down to the bottom. She had heard the dungeons mentioned so there was plenty of time.

The effort required in climbing the tower stairs suddenly seemed worth it.

I'll slip in behind him on the way down.

She leaned against the wall near the top of the stone staircase.

He was coming her way. He'd seen her. She smiled and so did he.

Sensational! Nearest description? Electric shock, she thought.

"Stephanie Beauchamp get a hold of yourself!"

He was three in front of her as they started the descent. He'd definitely noticed her and she had a clear view of him.

He wouldn't make the rugby team but there was plenty of strength there.

Clothes? Trendy. Not Stephanie's usual choice but...

They'd reached the large hall.

Mavis was prattling on. Good job it wasn't one of those earphone tours... they do nothing to promote togetherness.

She was alongside him now.

He turned and winked. Yes! He winked!

His eyes were... tawny.

Where had that word come from? Her father. That was how Mum had referred to the colour of his eyes. She'd inherited the blue.

She looked again. She felt good about him and herself.

He motioned her to silence. OK, speaking could come later when they were alone… even the thought sent a shiver through her. She was sure he fancied her.

He'd moved. Where?

Oh no! Surely he wasn't with them !

The two young men, who had been part of the 'singing' on the coach, were now closely 'exploring' the suits of armour. Their doubtful dramatic talents were emerging sending a subdued ripple of laughter through the company.

But, as she watched him, all negative feelings quickly disappeared.

Bit taller than I thought. Glad he's got a sense of humour.

"Please do not touch the exhibits."

The Voice had spoken and order was restored.

Stephanie caught a glimpse of Fiona who looked anything but amused. She obviously disapproved. There might be difficulties ahead for that friendship.

Now for the dungeons.

Hoping for a closer encounter… where better than in the dungeons?

Stephanie moved carefully, seeking space.

She knew he was somewhere behind and it wouldn't be easy for him to see her in the darkness.

Mavis was in her element recounting the gory details of those who had been incarcerated here.

Stephanie was only half listening. She was living for the moment.

She shivered. It was beginning to feel cold.

And then it happened!

The gentle touch on the shoulder and…"What's a nice girl like you doing in a place like this?"

Not the most original of introductions! But the voice was just perfect.

Trying to contain her eagerness, she slowly turned round, and found herself face to face with sweater, jeans and beard! Definitely not what she had expected or wanted.

Fortunately she was able to restrict her anger to a forcefully muttered, "Get lost!"

She determinedly stepped away and, despite the poor light, clearly saw him on the other side of the group. As she began moving in his direction he beckoned to her and indicated an even darker recess to his left. She was right, he did fancy her. If she could just make it round without too much fuss.

She could see now, the recess was actually a passage and he wanted her to follow him. The adrenaline was racing. All warning lights switched off.

"If you retrace your steps up the stairs and turn left you will come to the souvenir shop."

The spell was broken.

And with, "I hope you have enjoyed the tour and that your time in Warwick will prove very beneficial," Mavis began shepherding her flock back to the daylight.

At that moment Stephanie felt the desperate urge to condemn another woman to the dungeon tortures. Her timing couldn't have been worse.

A momentary lapse of her attention and he had gone.

Frantically she pushed her way through the group to get to the stairs. She hadn't even got his name.

She ignored the "Please go carefully," entreaties.
Where was he?

"There you are Steff. Isn't this a great place? Just imagine what it must have been like…"

Stephanie wasn't listening.

Where was he? He must have been in front of her when that silly woman had said, well, whatever she said, but she couldn't see him now.

"I've got another picture for my collection," Fiona was still going on.

"He's a dream. Sounds as if he scored with every woman he met too!"

Stephanie looked at the postcard thrust in front of her and froze.

She had found what she was looking for.

She read the inscription, "Richard Beauchamp, Earl of Warwick, 1389-1439."

"With looks like that he'd be hard to resist!"

"Completely irresistible," was all Stephanie could manage.

All on a Summer's Day

It had been a good day. George settled down behind the wheel. All that remained was a leisurely drive home. This was one of his regular holiday 'day trips.' The car knew the route, the scenic route, so well that George said it could virtually drive itself back. He smiled at the picture of the rather elderly Ford Focus negotiating the return journey on auto-pilot. No, better still, flying over the countryside like Chitty Chitty Bang Bang. That was a nice film and George was a nice person.

He began humming to himself. "Yes. It had been a good day."

The annual visit to Weston was a sort of pilgrimage in remembrance of long ago family seaside holidays; happy memories tinged with the inevitable sadness.

George's life was routine, as was the way his annual leave was spent in 'day trips. Colleagues in the office would certainly endorse the 'nice man' picture, confessing to the occasional smile at his expense whilst always maintaining the height of propriety to his face.

Moving with the job had been one of the most daring decisions in George's life. Securing the maisonette had taken such courage, leaving the security of the Midlands' base. The West Country had proved just enough attraction. The fact that the estate agent had been born just seven miles from Stafford had helped to steady his nerves. Everything seemed to have worked out for the best and George felt well and truly settled.

He glanced in the mirror. It was going to be a lovely sunset.

"Red sky at night." Another fine day tomorrow. It would be sensible to visit the bird garden just in case there was change in the weather on Thursday. He could wait and decide in the morning. He should be home in time to watch the news and he could check the weather forecast.

It was at this moment that George's life took a sudden turn.

Rounding the bend... It would be hard to find words to describe his reaction to the scantily dressed female in the middle of the road. The female was jumping about waving her arms and shouting.

He had to stop There was no way round.

He felt heat rising and recalled a not too dissimilar sensation when he had bought the wrong paper and on opening it had been confronted with... well not too different a picture from what he saw, live, in front of him.

Bending down in the pretence of adjusting the handbrake, George suddenly felt the urgent desire to pray to any God who might come to his aid.

The female came to the side of the car, and still talking, or rather babbling incoherently, proceeded to open the door and start to pull him out. She didn't seem in the least embarrassed at her lack of conventional attire.

George took a deep breath. The lady was in distress and believed, rightly or wrongly, that he, George could do something about it.

With great self-control, he placed a hand on her arm in an attempt to calm her down, and, smiling, indicated that he would lock the car and follow.

She continued to go on and on. If only she had been French he could have said something, but it wasn't French, more likely something Scandinavian if he had to make a guess.

They negotiated the gate and began to cross the field, sort of together.

Miss X, as his little grey cells had labelled her, made a series of small running forays, gesticulating wildly with vigorous arm and body movements to accompany the non-stop barrage of words.

George followed at an appropriate pace. He found it very difficult to know just where to look. Vainly he searched for clues amongst the words and actions. The nearest he could get was a robbery, apparently perpetrated by something from outer space, but it seemed rather unlikely in the Somerset countryside!

A near miss with a cow-pat introduced the idea of a bull. He tried to imitate a horned creature attacking but Miss X showed no recognition; perhaps his miming was a little lacking.

The field was uneven and sloped somewhat.

A little in the rear of his companion, George had a breakthrough. He observed water glistening on the long blond tresses in front of him. Got it! Someone had fallen in the river and he was being called to the rescue. At this time of year, he knew that, 'river' was somewhat of an exaggeration so there was no need to panic. George had watched a recent rescue series and he quickened his step. He was actually beginning to feel he could cope allowing space of thought… when he saw the caravan. It had been hidden until they rounded the blackberry bushes.

George's mind raced… and so did Miss X, physically, to the caravan steps. Still talking but fortunately no longer flapping, she pulled at the door handle and nothing happened. The door was locked. Or rather the door would not open. So that was it!

I will not bore you with details of what happened next. Suffice to say it took about twenty minutes for George to retrace his steps, collect the necessary tools from the car, and allow Miss X to regain access. He was completely overcome by her display of gratitude as she flung her arms round him, kissing him repeatedly on both cheeks. He was only able to make his escape after allowing her to take his photograph.

It was as he crossed the field for the fourth time that the question arose in his mind as to how the caravan actually got there in the first place… he certainly hadn't noticed a car.

In the morning, all previous plans were waived.

George spent the day getting over the excitement, only venturing out to walk to the newsagent's to buy his local evening paper.

One could suggest that it was a little unfortunate for George that Gerda's absent companion was a local journalist, away covering a story at the time of the happening.

You may be one step ahead of me!

The picture on the front page! Somehow... and George would be the first to admit that the ways and means of modern printing were beyond him... there he was, together with the curvaceous Miss X.

And in very large letter the heading:

INTERNATIONAL FRIENDSHIP...
ACTIONS SPEAK LOUDER THAN WORDS.

"Very nice too Lucky old Mr Simpson!" the voice came from behind the counter.

And almost immediately from alongside him another voice, "You'll have trouble livin' this one down mate!"

George turned towards the speaker and... because there was absolutely nothing he could possibly say... he just smiled.

Called to Account

"I'm sorry. I don't know what else to say. It's all so awful."

I glanced at him. No obvious response.

"It's all gone wrong. I never meant it to be like this."

Still nothing.

"It wasn't an easy decision to leave you know. I didn't really want to hurt Geoffrey. God! I tried! The letter to the newspaper was a bit naughty though."

He's waiting. Get a hold of yourself woman! You have a right to speak up for yourself. Be honest: no one else will be interested in your side of the story.

Tell him.

"I'd like to try to explain but it's quite a long story."

He spoke for the first time.

"Take your time. No rush."

He beckoned me to the chair at his side.

"My time is yours. Begin when you feel ready."

The warmth of his voice gave me the confidence I needed.

"Ours was a student romance. I was instantly attracted to Geoffrey. He had everything. I don't mind telling you,

I set out to get him. My ego rocketed sky high when Geoffrey seemed interested. Things went well. I decided very quickly that this was it. I suppose the fact that I was at Art College and he was training for the Ministry should have rung some bells, but I was in love and nothing else mattered. I realise now how one-sided the romance element must have been.

I've listened so often to Geoffrey say "If anyone knows of any just cause why these two persons… " and experienced the inner urge to scream "Yes, yes, yes!" And, with the devil in me surfacing, add "Sprouts!"

Small, round, green sprouts!

My mother had always insisted they were good for me. Goodness knows what Geoffrey's mother had said to bring about his obsession. Over the years I had meekly accepted the unwritten law that every Sunday roast should be accompanied by sprouts.

I've grown them, picked them, cleaned, debugged and cooked them; served them and, under sufferance, eaten them. I have prepared sprouts for numerous church meals and admired their excellence at the annual produce show. Out of season, the freezer has provided. My one enjoyable sprout experience each year has been to uproot the overgrown plants and exterminate them on the compost heap uttering ever stronger words of committal!

Sorry about the outburst. I've wanted to say that for years.

I don't want you to think that our time together has been all bad… far from it. I could share so much but I want to try to link it all to yesterday.

I suppose I came to see sprouts as a symbol of the sacrifice of my personal identity.

We moved twice during our marriage. Each time I hoped things might be a bit different but, of course, they weren't. Geoffrey was becoming more and more boring. I know it's my fault really. I should have realised. But… you don't do you?

My life was just drifting and I let it.

The advertisement in the library jumped out at me.

Geoffrey said it sounded fine. He had a regular meeting anyway so it wouldn't affect him.

Very quickly the Wednesday Art Class became the highlight of my week.

The company of like minds, where age didn't matter, revolutionised my life. I was accepted in the group as ME and it felt wonderful. Techniques, ideas, colour, everything just happened.

One week Jane invited me to come for a birthday celebration drink. I hesitated at first but it was the beginning of the social extra.

Geoffrey never questioned the fact that I came home so much later and I saw no reason to disclose unsolicited information.

Wednesday evening reintroduced life with a capital "L" and I became more and more dissatisfied. Conflict raged between my situation and what the rest of the world offered. I needed space. I had to do something.

The vision came suddenly.

Looking at my still life, I clearly saw cups, jug and teapot overflowing with sprouts. Honestly it was as if

I'd painted them in. Probably a revelation of my true nature.

I began planning it all in my mind.

Sunday's sprouts were both the last straw and the green light.

Little did Geoffrey know what his complaint about the soggy, overcooked mess would initiate.

Monday's regional diocesan meeting handed me a clear day.

Purchasing sacks of sprouts provided no obstacle. I spread my buying of course and found people only too delighted to offload produce.

On return home I filled everything with sprouts. I remember experiencing a chaotic mixture of emotions. I actually laughed out loud as I pictured the look of utter disbelief on Geoffrey's face as at every turn he came face to face with his beloved sprouts.

The anonymous note through the newspaper office suggesting an interesting story at the vicarage on Tuesday was a last minute idea.

I shut my case and fastened the strap. As I slung my painting satchel over my shoulder, I remember wondering whether I meant this to be forever. I don't think I'd made a final conscious decision. I was totally absorbed gloating over the success of my master plan and the chance to get my own back.

Geoffrey has another weakness: his inability to live up to his preaching; "See a need and act." Even the smallest repair job remains unattended!

In my state of elation I had completely forgotten the loose stair carpet.

"You know the rest. It's all so unexpected."
"It often is."
St. Peter rose from his seat and offered me his hand.
"Thank you for being so honest."
And together we walked towards the Gates.

Mix and Match

First impressions might lead one to believe that Cora was just like any other senior citizen. Those close to her however, always conscious of the sparkle in her eye, would remark, "With Cora, expect the unexpected." Since her retirement, there was even more time available for Cora to demonstrate that life, with all its pressures, needed to be relaxed by fun times.

But she did fit the pensioner picture to some degree. She was definitely a creature of habit. For example, unless something out of the ordinary took her away from home, her evening meal each day would be followed by coffee and the crossword in the local paper, the cryptic version. Monday, March 27th followed her usual pattern.

It was while she was gradually filling in the blank squares, rejoicing that today's clues contained a considerable number of anagrams, that the latest moment of inspiration came. An idea had been around for some time… nothing to do with crosswords really… and it all just suddenly came together. New ideas arrived in the most unexpected ways.

She had to telephone immediately. It couldn't wait.

Of course he wasn't there so she left a brief explanatory message for James and asked him to call back with his thoughts as soon as possible.

Returning to the hastily cast aside paper Cora found it very difficult to concentrate, Her mind was buzzing and, when set in motion, Cora's mind, about to enter its seventieth year, was more than a match for considerably younger specimens. She didn't have to wait for the go ahead, she could set things in motion first thing in the morning.

Martin would not have expected that an elderly, grey haired woman would be his first customer. She wanted a sleeping bag... nothing particularly strange about that... she was probably buying a present for some young relation. It was when she rummaged in her large handbag, produced a woolly hat and placed it on her head requesting a colour match that the word eccentric sprang to mind. Hardly pausing for breath, she added that she wanted one of those 'roll-up ones,' small and easy to carry as well as able to keep her super warm. Then he really began to wonder about her. The thought crossed his mind that this just might be a 'set up' to test his salesman skills, so following the unwritten law that the customer is always right, he politely excused himself to look in the stock room. Managing to maintain his composure, he returned with an item he thought would fit the bill. Unrolled, held up against herself, carefully viewed in the changing room mirror and the sale was made.

The final comment from his smiling, satisfied, customer left him wondering even more.

"Thank you. It will blend in perfectly with ageing Bath stone."

He'd have to share this one with Julie at lunchtime.

Clutching the carrier bag clearly displaying to the world that, "Tindalls is the Best for all Outdoor Pursuits," Cora waited in the queue at the tourist information desk.

In front she easily identified two oversized Americans and a group of Japanese. The two young men immediately ahead of her were arguing in a language she didn't recognise. The assistant was on the phone, she'd have to be patient.

Cora glanced around. Lots of information about what was on offer for the tourist. Plenty of items for sale up the other end, temptation that contributed greatly to the finance of this heritage city. It all fitted in well.

Argument apparently over, the two young men had moved away and,with the American's sorted, the young assistant was dealing with the oriental visitors. Cora smiled as she wondered how her request would be coped with. She didn't have to wait long to find out.

"I'd like to book in for one of the night watches in the Roman Baths please?"

Response? The young woman just stood looking at her.

Then, as if suddenly brought back to life, she smiled and said,

"I'm not sure what you mean. The Baths close each evening at 9pm. They're not open at night."

"But I've bought a sleeping bag like my friend said." Cora placed the carrier bag on the counter and waited.

Remaining remarkably calm, Fiona, her name clearly displayed on her badge,continued speaking, "If you'll just wait a moment Madam, I'll check it out with the manager. It may be something new that I haven't heard about."

She'd handled it well. Good advertisement for the city. The name badge also made the encounter somewhat more personal. Cora wondered if 'whoever he was,' would come and speak personally. She doubted it. In her experience, managers usually managed to remain hidden.

Fiona returned and informed her that they hadn't received any information about night sessions at the Baths but they'd be happy to check it further and pass on details if she'd like to leave a contact number.

Aware of a considerable queue forming behind her, Cora quickly wrote her name and telephone number on the piece of paper presented, and left graciously. There was plenty more she could have said but, in the circumstances, she decided to leave it at that.

By the time she reached home, after beans on toast at her favourite café, there were two messages on the answer-phone.

Message 1: "Aunt Cora, its Sam. Lovely to hear from you. I'll go along with your idea. Email it to me as soon as possible. You never cease to surprise me! Will try to speak to you later. Bye."

Message 2: " Howard Jones, Tourist officer leaving a message for Cora Bartlett at approximately 12.35pm. The Roman Baths confirm that they have no plans to open to visitors at night. The person who gave you that information must have imagined it all. Sorry we can't help."

The afternoon was spent in front of the computer. After a considerable number of rewrites, the requested item was on its way, well before Cora's dinner, coffee and crossword time.

The next morning was telephone time for Cora.

"Council offices. How can I help you?"

"Could you connect me to the cleansing department please?"

"Certainly. Just hold the line."

"Health and cleansing. Sue speaking."

"I wonder if I could speak to Mrs Constance Emall please."

"How are you spelling that?"

"E M A double L. She might shorten her Christian name to Con."

"Will you hold the line please and I'll check our files."

Cora waited, music filling the space between them.

"I'm sorry to have kept you waiting. I'm afraid I can't find any record of an employee by that name. Are you sure you've got the right department?"

"I'm pretty sure she worked in the Roman Baths area. That would be you wouldn't it?"

"Perhaps she uses a maiden name or something but I'm afraid I can't help."

"Never mind. Thank you for trying. Now can you connect me to the archaeological section or do I need to go back through the switchboard?"

"I can do that for you. Just hold the line."

More gap music.

"Heritage Centre. Amanda speaking."

"I was hoping to speak to Professor Wright, Leslie Wright please."

"We don't have anyone by that name here."

"But you're the archaeology department aren't you?"

"Not strictly. We're the Heritage Consultation

Centre. Perhaps your professor is part of the University Archaeology Faculty. Shall I give you their number?"

"Would someone there be consulted if a problem arose in the city?"

"Could be. Perhaps we might be able to help if you could give me a few more details."

"That's very kind of you but I think I'll try to have a word with Les if you could give me that number."

"Certainly. It's 01225 of course, 832728. I hope you find him. Can't say I've come across that name myself."

"I'll give it a try. Thank you for your help."

Cora replaced the receiver.

Should she or shouldn't she make a further call? It wasn't strictly necessary but another contact would be worth it.

It was hardly surprising that they'd never heard of Professor Les Wright, but there was no doubt that the young woman on the end of the line was interested in there being something of concern connected with the Baths.

Just one more short call to find out the opening times at the zoo for tomorrow and a very satisfactory morning's work was complete.

Cora hadn't been to Bristol Zoo for years. She parked on the downs. The forecast had suggested scattered showers but it wasn't cold.

Once inside so many memories came flooding back. As a child she had loved coming to this place. That was before any questions arose about the cruelty of caging wild animals. She knew of the excellent conservation work being undertaken here together with several research projects and that helped to suppress any guilt feelings. But she was here on business. "Business first; self indulgence later," she told herself as she made straight for the Nocturnal House.

The Nocturnal House hadn't been there during her childhood visits. As she entered and allowed her eyes to get accustomed to the darkness, Cora admitted to herself that she would probably have been too scared to come in as a child. A school group was gathered round a keeper with a lamp. He was talking about bats… incredible… just what Cora wanted. The large glass area behind him was full of bats of various sizes and species. Some were hanging upside down from stark branches, all perfectly still, while the rest crisscrossed the area, with rapid fluttering movement. It was almost unbelievable, to anyone observing, that there was never a hint of collision in such a confined space.

The lecture had finished; the children were moving; now was her opportunity.

"Do you have any hornam bats here?"

The young man turned to Cora, "I'm sorry…"

"I just asked if you had any of the very rare hornam bats here."

"Can't say I've ever heard of that species. What is their country of origin?"

"Possibly South America, but I'm not really sure. All I know is they're very rare."

"They must be. We've got a pretty wide range of specimens here but there are definitely no horam one's amongst them."

"It's hornam… not horam. Strange. I would have thought any ornithologist would have heard of them."

Daniel felt that his day, which had not started well, was deteriorating rapidly. He now had to decide whether to point out the difference between birds and bats to this obviously 'batty' old woman or escape by allowing her comment to just pass him by. The latter idea won hands down.

However during the rest of the day he casually tested out his apparent lack of knowledge with a number of other people with completely negative results. He even made a mental note to check out the internet when he got home.

Cora, mission accomplished, spent the rest of the day wandering around the pathways, visiting the various animal houses and reliving the happiness of the past.

Her happiness was complete when, for the first time this week, she actually finished the crossword.

Friday was supermarket morning. There was very seldom anything that occurred during this weekly visit that might, even vaguely, be described as exciting. A few snippets of conversation overheard at the checkout had been known to spark off ideas, not to mention the occasional difference of opinion in the car park, but really it was just one of those necessary chores that had to be endured. Cora's main desire was to get the whole day over in her anticipation of the next morning.

She managed to fill the afternoon with cake making, ironing and writing a long overdue letter to her cousin Amy.

An uneventful day concluded with an easy salad meal. The solution of one clue in the crossword eluded Cora; perhaps an evening's 'whodunit' with Miss Marple would provide some lateral thinking. Agatha Christie had a habit of coming up with the unexpected. As she settled comfortably in front of the television, she couldn't help hoping that she would be the author of a few surprises in the morning.

Cora walked round early to get a paper.

Her hand was shaking with excitement as she handed over payment. She could see it. He'd put it on the front page under the bold heading, 'TOURISM BONUS.' She stood outside the shop and read the article.

> *There will be an added attraction for visitors to the heritage city of Bath this summer. A colony of hornam bats has been discovered in the Roman Baths area. These previously unseen mammals are creating quite a stir.*
>
> *The discovery was made when Mrs Constance Emall, a council cleansing operative, was accidentally shut in at closing time.*
>
> *Con said, "I must have fallen asleep while I was working. When I woke up it was dark." She went on to describe how she heard a whirring sound and saw small creatures flying around in the steam behind the hot spring. Con added, "I reported it first thing. Well you never know. One hears strange things about flying things, diseases and all that!"*
>
> *Professor Les Wright, an eminent archaeologist, checked out the site the next day. He said, "I was amazed*

when I realised that what we had here was no ordinary bat. It's very exciting. I can't imagine how this news will be received in ornithological circles. Visitors will come from all corners of the world."

This discovery is seen as a great new source of revenue for the city. The tourist board are, at present, examining ways of promotion through sound recordings.

Early bookings to view can be made now. All that is needed is a sleeping bag, your own mug with coffee or tea bag since hot water is in constant supply, and a lot of gullibility.

It was all there, just as she'd planned it. Having your nephew as the editor of the local paper was not without its benefits.

Rereading the article back home, Cora wondered just how many people would be taken in by the Roman Baths in their new shape or how many would be aware of today's date. As she thought of the way she'd trailed the idea during the past few days, at very least, a few bells might just start to ring. She smiled. It had been fun. She'd enjoyed setting it up and she hoped that the article would evoke a few smiles for others.

Today she'd tackle the crossword with her morning coffee and, who knows, inspiration just might come as to some further use for an easily transportable, super warm sleeping bag!

A Very Nice Man

"I'll endeavour to get you to the Eiffel Tower before 2 a.m. when they switch off the floodlights. It's one of the things I always try to do. Perfect way to finish off the holiday week don't you think?"

Amid the general hum of gratitude and anticipation my inner voice responded quite differently.

"Perfect for you perhaps Mike, anything but for me!"

I wanted to scream, "No! No! No!"

Mike had been wonderful, enabling us all to feel at ease. Smooth driving, pointing out places of interest in the daylight, playing mood assisting background music as the sun set, always on hand to give assistance with entering or leaving the coach, and somehow possessing an uncanny way of knowing just the right moment to stop for a break. If ever there was a man cut out for his job, Mike was that man.

How could he know that this final act of kindness would ruin everything for me?

Doris had decided that journey time couldn't be wasted just sitting. I had come to realise that time wasting, as she called it, didn't exist at all for Doris, not even on holiday. Today, from the moment of departure, she was elsewhere in the land of her paperback.

I was glad to have this time to cope with my thoughts.

Doris is a seasoned traveller. We had met as we waited for the coach at Victoria. She seemed to sense my nervousness and had taken me over when she discovered that this was my first solo holiday. 'Taken over' is rather unkind for Doris had actually enabled me to get full value out of this trip to Spain and it has been so good never to find myself sitting alone. She must have had a good effect on me because towards the end of the week I had felt confident enough to join in conversation with other members of the group.

Jack would be proud of me!

Now with Mike's words echoing round my ears I turned to my unseen, but ever present, companion.

What can I do Jack? Help me!

The answer seemed to come as clearly as if he was sitting beside me,

"You can always stay on the coach."

Of course. Why hadn't I thought of that?

Jack had always had the answers.

I felt calmer. I settled back to enjoy the passing countryside.

"Have you ever been to Paris?"

Taken by surprise, I whirled round to find Mike standing behind my chair.

Food and drink consumed, Doris was now in the service station shop.

I was on my own.

Paris! Of course I'd been to Paris.

Why couldn't he leave me alone?

"Answer him Sue. He's only asking a question."

There he was again, my unseen resource.

"Yes." And after a slight pause I added, "but it was a long time ago."

"We've made good time so far but you can never tell when a hold-up might occur. I'll keep my fingers crossed." He smiled. "Not when I'm driving!"

He left me.

I watched him moving from table to table fulfilling his role to the end.

He really did have a nice smile. He'd been smiling all the week. Even when there had been the odd confrontation he never seemed to lose his cool. He was a nice man. Bet his wife missed him when he went away for these long trips.

I had missed Jack when he had worked away. Nothing like I missed him now!

I wondered whether it would be worth praying for a traffic hold-up so that we could go straight to the ferry. I had an overwhelming urge to get home.

O.K. I know that's not on.

I looked at the thin gold band and whispered… but I'm not sure I can cope!

"How would you like to be, down by the Seine with me?"

The tape announced our arrival in the French capital.

Doris deserted me and her book, and moved nearer to

the front of the coach to renew her acquaintance with the sights of the city.

Paris was alive even at this time of night.

Street lights replaced daylight almost unobtrusively.

There was the river, the boats, Notre Dame… all there as I remembered it.

"Under the bridges of Paris with you."

The music said it all!

The previous impenetrable veil was only just holding up. The floodgates were being severely tested.

We joined the procession along the Champs Elysees.

Moving so slowly.

Goodness! The café was still there but it didn't look the same.

"I love Paris in the springtime."

It was getting worse!

I turned away from the window. Nothing was the same.

Ahead was the magnificent Arc de Triomphe. I felt anything but triumphant.

The coach came to a halt and Mike's voice replaced Sasha Distel.

"Made it with twenty minutes to spare. Everybody out!"

My legs took over.

Before I realised, I was up and moving out into the cold night air.

I must have switched to autopilot!

It was as my eyes travelled upwards that the tears finally came.

I moved into the shadow by the side steps. I had to be on my own.

Why? Oh why had I come on this beastly trip? I had begun to cope so much better but now it was all ruined. It was as bad as it had ever been.

And then I saw Mike and the large white handkerchief.

Mike! How blind I'd been! Wrapped up in my own problems while all the time Mike... I felt drawn towards him.

"You too. I never realised."

Without looking up he said, "I try to come here each trip to let Joan know I'm alright. It was one of our places." He paused. "It's gradually getting easier."

We stood together in silence. Words would have been an intrusion.

The lights went out and we moved towards the waiting coach.

Mike smiled and said, "You ought to come to the Blackpool Lights trip in September... unless that's another of your problem places."

And in the darkness I heard another voice saying,

"He really is a very nice man."

The Meeting

Paula ran and reached the shelter of the doorway before the full force of water was released from the now leaden sky. Her carefully chosen dress was damp but not soaked. Rain hadn't featured in her plan for the day. There was certainly plenty of room for a small umbrella in the carrier bag. She risked a smile.

"If you take an umbrella you can be sure it won't rain." Words she'd heard so often from her mother but today was her day, her mind had been filled with far more important things than the weather. She rummaged in her handbag and found the small packet of tissues. Each tissue rapidly became a soggy mess as she tried to dry her legs. Moving downwards towards her ankles she was aware of the spurts of water beyond her sandaled feet as raindrops hit the pavement with considerable force. Her attention was drawn along to where a small cascade descending from the corner overhang was running towards the gutter and she realised she was not alone. Another pair of feet had joined her in the recess. Where had they come from? More to the point, what she saw in no way encouraged her to investigate their owner.

Had circumstances been otherwise she would have quickly moved on but that was not an option. She would have to wait here… even if it didn't stop raining she was actually very near her planned destination. She would have to make the best of it.

She moved the daffodils to one side and dropped the wet tissues into the carrier alongside the plastic box that contained the remains of her picnic lunch. She risked a quick glance to the left and her initial fears re the owner of the feet were confirmed! Male... age uncertain... scruffy clothes and... he smelt!

Not nice!

"Bloody rain!" Then, turning in her direction..."sorry ma'am."

Paula sort of muttered acceptance of the apology and edged further into her corner. She encouraged herself to stay calm but immediately cringed as her companion was racked with a bout of coughing that seemed to go on and on. It was horrible. Just as she was beginning to fear for his health the noise stopped as he partook of the contents of a bottle that he extracted from somewhere in the recesses of his dirt stained coat.

"Have a swig?" A tattooed hand extended the bottle towards her. "Warm you up."

Before she could make any response he took another swig and went on: "Nice dress. Bloody June! Sorry, done it again!" all in quick succession and then once more the offer to share.

"No thank you." She was tempted to add, "I don't drink and I'll tell you why," but that would have sounded judgemental. Her planned meeting could well prove confrontational... she didn't want to take any risks now.

"Suit yerself." He had another and then burst into song.

"I'm singin' in the rain… singin' in the rain… just singin' in the rain."

Pause. Another gulp.

"Bloody rain!"

Beginning to wonder if she could cope, Paula looked at her watch… ten past… hopefully not too long to wait. She had discovered quite by chance that her father was in Bath. She hoped her letter had reached him.

Thankfully the vocal was restricted to one line.

Silence.

Then he was off again.

"You on holiday?" He obviously wanted to talk. They'd been thrown together in a very unusual way, but this was a very public place and she could run if necessary.

"No I'm just here for the day."

"And you landed this bloody rain." She was aware of shoulders and head scrunched together, recognising that there would be a recurrent need for apology in any further conversation they might have together.

"Shame."

Despite his appearance, he really seemed quite nice. Paula wondered how old he was. She was glad that the doorway was quite wide as her nose became ever more sensitive.

"Come on the train?"

"Yes."

"Where from?"

Paula paused for a moment. Should she be having this conversation with a complete stranger? Surely there could be little danger and it would help to pass the time until what might lay ahead. But you had to be careful. If her letter had indeed reached its destination the meeting should happen around 7.30pm. In one way she wanted the remaining minutes to fly by but she was equally filled with apprehension.

Well, just reply then.

"Portsmouth."

"Pompey."

There was something in the way he said the word that caused Paula to give her companion full attention for the first time. Amongst the straggly hair on head and chin two eyes suddenly came alive.

"You can always tell by the eyes." Drat… her mother was intruding again.

"I was in the navy so I know Pompey. That was a good time in my life," adding somewhat wistfully, "A long time ago."

"You'd notice a difference now. You ought to pay a visit."

The words were out. Stupid, stupid, stupid! How was this 'down-and-out' going to manage to visit her city?

He didn't seem to notice but just continued,

"My daughter was born in Pompey… haven't bloody seen her for years," and then with a half laugh, "who knows I may even be a Granddad by now."

Paula shivered and not from the cold. If only he knew.

The flow of words stopped for a further visit to the whisky bottle.

She looked at her watch again and then sought confirmation from the large station clock at the end of the road. Not long now.

Would he come?

Across the road a few men had started to gather. She bent down and carefully adjusted the daffodils to be visible above the top of the bag. She'd congratulated herself on the idea of adding them into the plan, fitted in well, but somehow they felt different from when she'd left home.

"Are those daffodils real?" He was back in the present day.

"No they're artificial."

"I thought so. Wrong time o' year for daffodils. I went to the Isles of Scilly once picking early daffodils… spring flowers… my mother always used to say welcome sign of new life after the winter."

This man had a mother too. Of course he had but she'd never thought… suddenly he became a real person and she felt free to talk with him. Had they only met such a short time ago?

"When I was small I can remember my Dad getting a bunch of daffodils for me to give my Mum on Mothering Sunday."

Paula's time for remembering now.

She wanted him to know that what she described hadn't been a picture of love and gentleness. Somehow the experience of her small hand, clutching daffodils, being roughly grasped and thrust forward had stayed with her together with other unpleasant happenings. It still hurt like hell along with being reminded constantly that she was called Paula, the nearest he could get to the son she should have been. She hadn't realised about the alcohol then. She didn't think she'd ever known until he'd gone. At first there'd been the annual birthday and Christmas card but then nothing. In anger she'd planned the daffodils to see if he remembered. Did this man alongside even realise what day it was?

"Be bloody funny if some of the daffodils I picked were the ones you gave your Mum."

They both smiled.

"Meeting your boyfriend are you?" A complete freedom of exchange had developed.

As she responded with a shake of the head, he added,

"He's a bloody lucky fellow... wish I was a bit younger myself!"

Paula said nothing. There was nothing she could say.

He laughed again, then stretched, gave himself a bit of a shake, stamped his well sodden feet and moved forward to the pavement.

He looked up at the sky.

"Nearly stopped so I'll be on my way,"

A little more liquid refreshment, then he proffered his tattooed hand intended for shaking this time just as if their meeting had been in a completely normal setting.

"The name's Tom... nice to have met you."

Paula grasped the outstretched hand.

"And I'm Paula. Nice to have met you too Tom."

He didn't cross the road as she had expected. She watched briefly as he walked, somewhat unsteadily, up the road in the direction of the park... a rather tuneless rendering of "Play up Pompey" his parting gift.

Paula's attention was already elsewhere. The rain had certainly eased and her eyes now carefully observed the men opposite beginning to move from the pavement into the Night Shelter.

She waited.

Would she recognise him? They all looked so much the same.

Oh no!… as realisation dawned… her Dad might look just like Tom.

She had wanted him to come to meet his little daughter who was now a confident adult. She had described her distinctive dress. He couldn't miss her.

Strange, she'd arrived full of anger but all that had changed in the last half hour. Now she just wanted to say, "Happy Father's Day" to her Dad and perhaps receive a hug.

The time ticked by. The queue grew shorter as one by one the homeless men, seeking shelter for the night, disappeared down the steps.

Gradually it became clear that her plan had failed. He wasn't coming. Perhaps he had moved on.

There was a train at 8.15pm… it looked as if checking the timetable for later trains had been a waste of time.

The last of the homeless men had descended into the warmth below.

Paula crossed the road her attention drawn by what looked like flowers previously hidden by the waiting queue. A bunch of summer flowers, now well past their best, had been tied to the railings alongside a note,

"God bless Stan. Rest in Peace."

She stood for a moment.

Then, almost reverently, she took the bright yellow daffodils from her bag and added them to the tribute.

Her remaining tissues would have another use.

The meeting was over.

On Special Offer

It just didn't feel right.

The boys had told everybody about going to the hotel... correction... Tom had told everybody! James had been much more concerned about how Father Christmas would know where to bring the presents.

"Spending Christmas at home as usual?"

Kirsty had forgotten how many times she had encountered a moment of surprised response as she sort of mumbled, "No. We're going to a hotel in Weston-super-Mare this year."

David had coped fine.

"If that's what Mum and Dad want to give us, stop worrying about it."

They were so kind but she still had moments of wondering whether they thought their only son could have done better.

Henry didn't think he could have done any better than to decide to spend the last years of his life, however many that might mean, living at The Grange.

Weston was his place.

They'd always managed to fit in at least one family trip each summer.

He smiled. How times had changed. Now everybody

went off to amazing places for holidays, some he'd never even heard of. Why only the other day that woman from Nottingham had talked about her granddaughter going off to travel around the world. He remembered that at her age all he'd needed was to be out in the open air on a sunny day... heaven after a shift underground.

The family had moved south in the 40s, responding to the need for more workers in the Somerset pits. It had been a good move. Henry had worked with his father down the mine until it closed. The years in the mines undoubtedly contributed to his father's early death. His mother and sister were gone now. They'd been lucky to be allowed to stay on in the cottage so long seeing as it had originally gone with the job. Just how he could now afford to live in a hotel remained a mystery.

Henry's love of the open air seemed to have paid off. The staff speculated about his date of birth but nobody in the hotel actually knew his age. His eyes and ears were showing signs of wear but the way he and his trusted walking stick addressed the promenade almost every day gave evidence that his legs were standing up to the test of time. And a lot of people would subscribe to the fact of his tongue and memory remaining pretty well intact too.

Memories were the problem for Joyce.

She stood at the window gazing out across the bay.

"Why did I ever agree to come?"

She was alone. That said it all.

They had planned so much that they would do together and then the heart attack.

Alan had only been retired seven months.

Last Christmas all the family had been together… quite a rare occurrence. They had all been so happy and only a few weeks later came the bombshell.

The Cruse Bereavement Group support had been wonderful.

But now she wondered if she had been stupid to choose to join the few members spending Christmas together.

She knew she could have gone to any of the family but the thought of that had somehow felt worse and they certainly wouldn't have allowed her to stay alone so she had put her name down.

Being here was something else.

Her eyes searched the darkness for the sea, but inside she knew she was searching for the courage to survive the days ahead.

Ben had made a bold decision and he too was searching… searching for tolerance of his fellow workers and the stamina to cope with the demands of the chef.

His brain and personality were far better suited to university life than a busy hotel kitchen.

The choice to be here, or a similar establishment, was based purely on his need for money. He had resisted the temptation to join the party skiing in the French Alps. Resistance had called for extreme sacrifice. He liked skiing, he liked partying and he liked the people going. But for once he had chosen to face the reality of life. He could not afford to go.

He'd been given a very small room at the back of the hotel, perhaps it could be better described as a large cupboard, but it was sufficient. With all meals provided he should be able to considerably reduce his overdraft. He'd been told that all tips were pooled and shared, that should work to his advantage as he would have little chance of impressing visitors from his lowly kitchen position.

Immediately after the evening meal all the guests had met in the lounge, as requested, for the stocking hanging-up ritual. Clearly labelled stockings had been carefully pegged on the tinsel lines set either side of the fireplace and were now awaiting seasonal contents.

Henry had seen it all before but he always enjoyed the 'happiness feel' of the occasion He'd enjoyed talking to that young woman with the two boys. She seemed really interested in the stories of his days down the mine. He wasn't quite so sure about her husband though.

Henry went out for a walk as the twins went to bed.

It was a clear night with very little wind.

He'd put on his old boots just in case he felt like going down on to the sand but that hadn't happened so much lately. It would probably be just along to the old pier and back.

Then he'd have a nice sit by the fire in his favourite chair before going to bed.

With the boys in bed, Kirsty and David came back down to the bar for a quiet time together. Kirsty's pre-Christmas drink would be her usual lemonade and lime.

Alcohol and Christmas! a horror that haunted Kirsty each year.

Did anyone realise what it had been like?

Every year her father had spent Christmas drunk! Really drunk!

Raging and swearing until finally he slumped down in the chair.

The snoring! The smell! It had been awful.

She remembered always being dead scared of what might happen next.

How she had longed to be like other children.

Of course the drinking happened all the time but at Christmas it felt worse.

Relief came when, one day, he had upped and left them.

It had been hard but somehow she and her Mum had pulled through together.

Occasionally she did wonder if he was still alive but they never spoke about him. She was aware however that it wouldn't be long before the boys started asking more questions.

She didn't even know how much David realised. In many ways he was very sensitive but there were some things she couldn't bring herself to talk about, even with David.

The vegetables had arrived late.

Evidently every chef in the area had ordered fresh produce.

It was nearing midnight when Ben finally left the kitchen. As he crossed the hallway his attention was drawn to the manger scene in the alcove. He'd been a shepherd once… and sung the wrong words! He smiled.

His hands went to his pockets and the fingers of his right hand brought out… a sprout. The picture of the green mountain he had just left replaced all pleasant thoughts of school nativity plays. Anger and resentment welled up. What a way to spend Christmas Eve!

An idea came.

With great relish and purpose, he placed the small green object alongside the gifts of the three wise men and retreated to his 'cupboard.'

As he lay down on his bed sounds from outside confirmed that, for some, celebration had already started.

Tom and James were not asleep as their parents in the adjoining room supposed. This was the year Tom was going to check out Father Christmas. He'd listened to the scoffing of the older boys in the playground and he had discussed the matter with James.

Nobody would suspect that they were twins as they didn't look or act alike. However the combination of their different personalities could prove an asset. On this occasion James wanted to work it out and Tom provided the how and the courage necessary.

They had planned it together.

Seated comfortably in the office, George, the night porter, had responded mechanically to the 'Goodnight' from the young man leaving the kitchen. His attention held by what was happening on the television screen in front of him.

The film was so good that he was unaware of two small figures tiptoeing across the hall towards the lounge some time later.

From just inside the doorway Tom and James could see the lines of stockings.

They moved forward a little.

Good, he hadn't been! The stockings still looked flat and empty.

But they were now faced with the problem of waiting.

How long should they wait? And where would be the best place to hide?

The answers to these questions hadn't featured in the planning.

Surprisingly the answer came quite quickly as a sudden, deep throated, cough emanated from the chair pulled up by the fire.

They froze!

From where they stood they couldn't see who had coughed but… they could both see the black boots and they could both see the very unusual sort of stick hooked over the back of the chair, definitely the right sort of stick for prodding reindeer.

No word passed between them, just a look, and with 'twinned' understanding they were out and up the stairs.

Joyce couldn't sleep.

She had heard a clock somewhere chime midnight but sleep didn't come.

She tried to blame eating more than she was used to late in the evening but she knew the real reason.

Nothing would ever be the same.

It hadn't helped that she had missed the midnight service. It had always been so much a part of Christmas. As young people it had provided an excuse to stay out late, one of the first occasions when Alan had walked her home.

None of the group had actually mentioned going to church so she had kept quiet. She didn't want to upset them when they had been so kind.

And then she remembered. When they arrived, she had noticed a nativity scene set out near the bottom of the stairs and she'd promised herself a closer look but it had gone out of her mind.

She could greet Christmas Day as usual.

In her blue dressing gown and slippers, and grasping the room key tightly, she made her way along the well-lit corridor and down the stairs.

George remained unaware of yet another visitor to his hall area.

Joyce moved round to the alcove and bent down to share in the wonder of the first Christmas depicted before her.

She read, "It came upon a midnight clear." Tears began to form.

Then she saw it… the small green sprout nestling beside the manger.

What was a sprout doing there? A sprout… one of the 'special things' between her and Alan.

Sprouts! Even the word brought a smile to her face.

"Alan! How could you?" The words fell out.

And suddenly it all came together… the gift… the love…Christmas.

She stretched out her hand and picked up the sprout.

"Thank you Alan," she said, and, with a new found confidence, made her way back upstairs.

The film ended and George thought it was time he made his rounds of the building.

In the lounge he found Henry fast asleep in front of a now completely extinct fire.

He gave the sleeping figure a gentle shake.

"Come on old chap, long past your bedtime."

George allowed Henry time to 'come to' and then assisted him to stand.

"Don't want to be here when Santa comes down the chimney do you now?"

He unhooked Henry's walking stick and handed it to him. Nice bit of workmanship that, excellent carving. Reminded him of…no never mind.

"I'll come up in the lift with you old fellow. I'm doing my rounds anyway."

Exhausted, but content, Kirsty had fallen asleep. She would do her best to relax and enjoy every moment of this time of celebration.

In the early light of Christmas Day she turned over and stretched out her hand towards her husband.

She stifled a scream.

Whatever was it? She recoiled back to her side of the bed. Help!

Wide awake, but refusing to let her eyes open, the question came again, "What on earth was it?"

Curiosity finally got the better of her.

There, sitting bolt upright in the middle of the bed, was a dog…a large dog… a large pink fluffy dog!

But? Unuttered questions came tumbling out.

"Happy Christmas Kirsty."

Kirsty didn't know who to hug first, David or the wonderful pink dog with the 'oh so soft' fur.

"Like it?"

The threesome clung together with kisses exchanged by the non-furry couple. Through her tears Kirsty managed a "How did you know?" before burying her face again.

"Better ask Father Christmas," came the answer.

Next door two young boys were no longer bothered about 'Hows?' or 'Whys?'

They had what they needed.

A banner, stretched across the room, displaying in large bright letters the message, "Presents left safely in the wardrobe and the bottom drawer.

Happy Christmas from 'You know who!'

Ben woke up in a surprisingly good mood considering how early it was. This was Christmas Day and he was going to do his best to approach everything and everybody in a very positive manner. He knew the first thing he must do. He felt ashamed and intended to remove the evidence of last night's anger. He should never have allowed himself to put the sprout by the manger. He would retrieve it before anyone noticed.

But it wasn't there. Someone had got there first…but who? All he knew was that he would be chief suspect in line for retribution. To keep his mobile switched on in his pocket, in the hope that he just might be remembered, laid him open to even more trouble.

But why worry?

Everything would be OK. After all it was Christmas!

"Christmas was and is a time for surprises."

Revd Timothy Wakefield could find no reason to suppose that this year would be any different.

He had once again shared in the mystery at the midnight gathering and now he was on his way back to the church for the Family Service.

He knew he would see people he never saw during the rest of the year but that didn't matter. It was quite sufficient that they wanted to add this bit to their Christmas celebration. There would be children wanting to show new toys, which would provide entertainment and, no doubt, extra noise for the occasion.

He would enjoy it all.

As he approached The Grange he glanced at his watch. Later on he would, once again, be amongst the guests enjoying Christmas dinner in this friendly place, but there was time now to just pop in and exchange seasonal greetings with whoever was working in reception.

The tastefully decorated foyer felt warm and welcoming, and the background music added to the happy buzz around the place.

Henry was moving towards him clasping a small, wel-filled stocking in one hand, while the other gripped his good strong walking stick. Timothy wasn't sure whether he'd recognise him; he seemed to have aged quite considerably lately.

"A very happy Christmas to you," the greetings spread around.

Two more bulging red stockings raced past and up the stairs, Tom and James were almost bursting with excitement.

A bright pink something, which shouted of Father Christmas, was being shown the manger scene in the alcove.

He smiled, and turned to go.

Yes! There would be surprises again this year, but he was glad that some things remained the same.

The special something that Christmas could offer to everyone, he knew that would never change, thank goodness!

And as a Post Script...

I am sending you a letter... a purely fictional letter!

You will, I hope, discover that it is full of sentences or, in some cases, just phrases, behind which lurk all sorts of story possibilities... people, places and experiences (where have I heard that before?)

As you read, I suggest that you allow your imagination to 'run riot.'

And then...who knows... you may feel inspired to share your thoughts... pick up a pen or embrace your computer... and actually explore your potential as an author.

Come to think of it, I feel sure there are plenty of ideas here for me to attempt to compile another book myself!

Dear Reader,

Many thanks for the loan of your apartment; it is just what I needed. The decision to have a 'get away from it all place' was an excellent idea.

I left the keys where I found them. I never did discover what the small one opened.

Ever since my unfortunate car park experience, I have been anti lifts, but on this occasion the stairs caused no problem.

To place an antique mirror opposite the front door is a master touch. My first impression was that someone had followed me in, but when I turned round there was no one there, must have been a trick of the light.

On the mat, I found an envelope simply addressed, "VINCENT URGENT!" Who, I wonder is Vincent?

Wednesday morning, winter sunshine, well wrapped up, and I was off. An hour up by the round tower with a view of The Solent was perfect.

I read the dedication on the back of the seat, "In loving memory of George Bartlett. He simply watched the waves."

I was alone and yet I suddenly felt embraced by the history of this great seaport. I followed the Millennium Rope Trail along the cobbled street until, like many others who had passed this way and in confidence that I would not be the last, I reached the 'Lively Lady.'

If I hadn't promised myself that men were definitely off the menu, I might have been tempted by the delicious guy behind the bar. Silently the blackboard menu said, "You must choose Fish."

The family in the corner caught my attention, very noisy, and definitely not English.

Vehicles were moving off the car ferry as I stepped outside; a mini-bus; a farm truck transporting animals; a prison van; fellow travellers now bound for very different destinations.

I took the short-cut back and noticed how everything looks so run down now, so sad. A black cat outside the door failed to trip me up as it rubbed around my boots in greeting, obviously a sign that my luck has changed. As one gets older areas of black and white blur into grey. I am aware not everything is quite what it seems, surprises prompt questions.

Even if I imagined the drift of smoke in the lounge, there is no doubt that the smell of tobacco pervaded the whole apartment for most of the evening.

I was woken during the night by the sound of breaking glass. In the darkness, I was aware that the walls were not soundproof and that the occupants of the next apartment were not sleeping peacefully.

I doubt if this is the sort of letter you might expect to receive, but you must know that a writer can be trusted to come up with the unexpected.

The train, the walk and the sea air seem to have unlocked my mind.

The outcome of my recent experience will be far reaching: you mark my words!

Love Barbara.

About the Author

BARBARA SHRUBSOLE

Barbara has been retired from primary school teaching for some time and enjoys writing as a hobby.

She moved from Portsmouth to Bath with her husband and family in 1975, and has three married children and seven, now adult, grandchildren.

Barbara is a member of Manvers Street Baptist Church and bases her life on practical Christianity.

She has always spent time in voluntary work and describes herself as a "people person."

At present she is involved in various ways within the Open House Centre.

Barbara has previously self published two books of poems but this is her first commercial publication.